THE BEAR

MORE PRAISE FOR
The Bear

"With artistry and grace . . . Krivak delivers a transcendent journey into a world where all living things—humans, animals, trees—coexist in magical balance, forever telling each other's unique stories. This beautiful and elegant novel is a gem."
—*Publishers Weekly* (starred review)

"A moving post-apocalyptic fable for grown-ups. . . . Ursula K. Le Guin would approve."
—*Kirkus Reviews* (starred review)

"Engagingly different. . . . Unfolds in graceful, luminous prose."
—*Library Journal* (starred review)

PRAISE FOR ANDREW KRIVAK

"Some writers are good at drawing a literary curtain over reality, and then there are writers who raise the veil and lead us to see for the first time. Krivak belongs to the latter." —**National Book Award judges' citation for *The Sojourn***

"[Krivak's] sentences accrue and swell and ultimately break over a reader like water: they are that supple and bracing and shining." —**Leah Hager Cohen**

"Incandescent." —**Marlon James**

"A writer of rare and powerful elegance."
—**Mary Doria Russell**

"Destined for great things." —**Richard Russo**

"[A] singular talent." —**Jesmyn Ward**

"An extraordinarily elegant writer, with a deep awareness of the natural world."
—*New York Times Book Review*

"[Krivak] bring[s] out the vast compassion, humanity and love of his rich, fully developed characters."
—*Star Tribune*

PRAISE FOR *The Sojourn*

**National Book Award Finalist
Chautauqua Prize Winner
Dayton Literary Peace Prize Winner**

"A story that celebrates, in its stripped down but resonant fashion, the flow between creation and destruction we all call life."
—**Dayton Literary Peace Prize judges' citation**

"A novel of uncommon lyricism and moral ambiguity that balances the spare with the expansive."
—**Chautauqua Prize committee citation**

"A gripping and harrowing war story that has the feel of a classic."
—**NPR.org "Year's Top Book Club Picks" citation**

THE BEAR

Andrew Krivak

Bellevue Literary Press
NEW YORK

First published in the United States in 2020 by
Bellevue Literary Press, New York

For information, contact:
Bellevue Literary Press
90 Broad Street
Suite 2100
New York, NY 10004
www.blpress.org

This is a work of fiction. Characters, organizations, events,
and places (even those that are actual) are either products of
the author's imagination or are used fictitiously.

Library of Congress Cataloging-in-Publication Data
Names: Krivak, Andrew, author.
Title: The bear / Andrew Krivak.
Description: First edition. | New York : Bellevue Literary Press, 2020.
Identifiers: LCCN 2018061687| ISBN 9781942658702 (trade paperback :
    alk. paper) | ISBN 9781942658719 (ebook)
Classification: LCC PS3561.R569 B43 2020 | DDC 813/.54--dc23
LC record available at https://lccn.loc.gov/2018061687

Bellevue Literary Press would like to thank all its generous donors—
individuals and foundations—for their support.

 This publication is made possible by the New York
State Council on the Arts with the support of Governor
Andrew M. Cuomo and the New York State Legislature.

This project is supported in part by an award
from the National Endowment for the Arts.

Book design and composition by Mulberry Tree Press, Inc.

Bellevue Literary Press is committed to ecological stewardship in our
book production practices, working to reduce our impact
on the natural environment.

∞ This book is printed on acid-free paper.

Manufactured in the United States of America.
First Edition

3   5   7   9   8   6   4   2

paperback ISBN: 978-1-942658-70-2
ebook ISBN: 978-1-942658-71-9

To Cole, Blaise, and Louisa

And to Amelia

*We did not guess its essence
until after a long time.*

—Ralph Waldo Emerson,
Essays: Second Series

THE BEAR

THE LAST TWO WERE A GIRL AND HER FATHER who lived along the old eastern range on the side of a mountain they called the mountain that stands alone. The man had come there with a woman when they were young and built a house out of timber, stones pulled from the ground, and mortar they made with a mix of mud and sand. It was set halfway up the mountain's slope and looked out onto a lake ringed with birch trees and blueberry bushes that ripened in summer with great bunches of fruit the girl and her father would pick as the two floated along the shore in a canoe. From a small window in front of the house—the glass a gift the woman's parents had given to her after having received it themselves from the generation before, so precious a thing had it become as the skill for making it was lost and forgotten—the girl could see eagles catching fish in the shallows of an island that rose from the middle of the lake and hear the cries of loons in the morning while her breakfast cooked over a hearth fire.

IN WINTER THE SNOWS BEGAN NOT LONG AFTER the autumn equinox and still visited the mountain months after the spring. Storms lasted for days and weeks at a time, drifts climbing up against the house and burying paths as deep as some trees grew high. Often the man had to wade for firewood or trudge out to his toolshed at the edge of the forest with a rope tied around his waist.

But when the winds settled, the skies cleared, and the low sun shone again, the man would wrap the young girl warm and tight in a pack, walk out into the stillness of winter, and float on snowshoes made of ash limbs and rawhide down to the frozen lake, where the two would spend the day fishing for trout and perch through the ice.

Snow covered so much of the girl's world from mountaintop to lake that for almost half the year all she could see when she looked out that window was a landscape at rest beneath a blanket of white.

AND YET NO MATTER HOW LONG WINTER LASTED, spring followed, its arrival soft and somehow surprising, like the notes of birdsong upon waking, or the tap of water slipping in a droplet from a branch to the ground. As the snow melted, black rocks, gray lichen, and brown leaf cover emerged from the once-uniform palette of the forest floor, and the thin silvery outlines of trees began to brighten with leaves of green against the groupings of hemlock and pine. Those were the days when the girl left the house in the morning with her father and studied a new world that pushed up from the dirt of the forest and emerged from the water at the edge of the lake, days in which she lay on the ground beneath a warm sun and wondered if world and time itself were like the hawk and eagle soaring above her in long arcs she knew were only part of their flight, for they must have begun and returned to someplace as of yet unseen by her, someplace as of yet unknown.

THERE WAS, THOUGH, ONE DAY AMONG ALL FOUR seasons of the year the girl loved best. The summer solstice. The longest day of the year.

The day on which the man told her she had
been born. And he made it a tradition to give
his daughter a gift on the eve of the solstice. She
didn't remember receiving the earliest ones,
but she cherished them just the same. A carved
wooden bird so lifelike, it looked as though it
could fly. A purse made of deer hide and sinew
that was her mother's and in which she kept col-
ored stones found along the lake. A water cup
shaped from a piece of solid oak and from which
she drank. A painted turtle that walked slowly
from the man's hands as he unfolded them and
which she kept for the summer as a pet, then
released down by the lake in the autumn.

On the eve of the year the girl turned five,
her father gave her a bowl of fresh strawberries
after their supper and said, I have a special gift
for you tonight.

He handed her a box made of birch skin,
around which a long piece of dried grass was
tied in a bow. She untied the bow and opened
the box. Inside was a silver comb polished
brightly and looking like nothing she had ever
seen before.

She stared at the comb for a long time, until the man broke the silence.

This was your mother's, he said. I have been waiting to give it to you. When I watched you fighting with your hair down on the lakeshore, I thought, This is the year.

She reached into the box, took out the comb, and held it as she would a thing delicate and to be revered.

I love it, she said quietly, closed her hand around the comb, then climbed into her father's arms and hugged him.

THE GIRL HAD HEARD THE VOICE OF THE MAN IN her ear for as long as she could remember, so she never wondered if there was someone else who might have once spoken to her as well. But when she was old enough to walk beyond the house and into the woods or down to the lake, she began to notice something about the animals. There were two foxes darting in and out of the downed-log den with their skulk of pups. Two loons escorted the baby loon across the deep middle of the lake every summer. And when she saw does grazing in spring in a small meadow at the base of the mountain, there were the fawns right by their sides. So after the girl had practiced running the comb through her hair and the man tucked her into bed and kissed her good night, she looked up at him and asked, Why are you alone?

The man knelt down at her bedside.

I'm not alone, he said. I have you.

I know, said the girl. I mean where did my mother go? Everywhere around me there are things you tell me were once hers. But she's not here.

She's here, he said. In what we remember of her.

But I don't remember her, she said. What happened to her?

The man bowed his head and lifted it again, and he told his daughter that when he and the woman buried their parents and came to the mountain and built their house, she was all the world he knew, and he believed for a time that the two of them would live alone in this world for the rest of their days. Until she discovered she was going to have a child.

Me, said the girl.

You, said the man. But when the time came, she had to struggle a great deal to bring you into the world. And after that struggle the only thing she could do was nurse you and rest. She was strong. Strong enough to live through the summer and into the fall to give you what milk and nourishment she had to give. But, in time, I knew she would leave us for that place where the struggle to bear a child had taken her, and neither you nor I could follow. And one evening before the hunter's moon she went to sleep and didn't wake.

The man turned away to look into the dark for a moment, then turned back to his daughter. She sat up and reached out from underneath the blanket and took his hand in hers.

It's all right, she said. I understand.

He smiled and said, You're a wise girl. But there's still much you can't understand. So much you shouldn't have to. Not yet.

Like what? she asked.

Well, like how even after all these years, years in which I've had you to think about every minute of every day, I still think of her. I still miss her and wish she were here.

The girl lay back down on the pillow.

Will I miss you one day? she asked.

One day, the man said.

The girl was quiet then and the man thought she might have fallen asleep, but she asked again into the dark, Are you sad that you have me instead?

Oh no, not for a moment! the man answered in a voice too loud for the room, and held the girl's hand tighter. Not for one moment. You see, you are the joy I have beyond any sadness or wish that remains for what once was. Without you . . .

His voice trailed off and he stared down at the floor, then back at his daughter.

Without you I'd be nothing but alone, he said.

And without you I'd be alone, said the girl.

A hint of moonlight had begun to creep with the summer dusk into the house through the window, and the man could see traces of the woman in the face of the girl.

I know what we'll do, he said. Tomorrow we'll climb to the top of the mountain where your mother is resting. She loved the mountain. She used to say the summit looked like a bear. I want you to see it, too. Would you like that?

Yes, said the girl.

Good, the man whispered, and kissed her on the forehead a second time and tucked her in tight. Then rest well. Tomorrow we have a big climb.

The girl rolled over and huddled beneath her blanket, and before the moonlight had left the window she was asleep.

SHE WOKE AT DAWN TO THE SONGS OF A GRAY catbird and walked into the kitchen, where her father was making a breakfast of dried apple slices and mint-leaf tea.

It's a beautiful morning, he said to his daughter. Eat and we'll go.

The girl rubbed her eyes and sat down at the table. She had awakened several times in the night and had not slept well. She had had a dream in which she was lost somewhere between the summit of the mountain that stands alone and home. But if she was uncertain about whether she could or even wanted to make the climb that morning, she kept these thoughts to herself. The man said her mother lay in the earth on the top of a mountain, and so she would try as hard as she could to get there for her as much as for him. She ate in silence, drank her tea, and filled a gourd with water. Then she put on her thick deerskin shoes for moving over rocks and said, I'm ready.

THERE WAS A PATH. NOT WORN BUT DISCERNIBLE. The first stretch of it was no more difficult than the walk to the house from the water's edge. As they climbed, though, the terrain became rockier, the trail steeper. By the time the sun had risen and the eastern and western shores of the lake were in full light, they had climbed with hands and feet up boulder after boulder to the midway point. There they rested on an outcropping of stone.

The girl drank water and ate a handful of hickory nuts. Her forehead was sweating and her legs ached, but there was no turning back. From what she could see from where they sat resting, the climb to the top looked harder than what she had just done.

The man wondered what was in her thoughts, and said, Your mother and I used to climb up here together every summer, but we were already grown by then. Do you know what that means?

The girl looked from the top of the mountain back at her father, and said, That I'm stronger than you.

Yes, the man said, and laughed. And I have a feeling you always will be.

He stood and shifted the contents of the pack in which he carried the things he always took when he left the house. Knife, flint and steel, bone needle and sinew line, tree nuts, and his own gourd filled with water.

We'll rest one more time, he said, and set off up the mountain.

His daughter rose and followed.

THEY REACHED A CRAGGY LEDGE AT THE BASE OF the summit after noon, by the man's reckoning. The air was cool, the sky cloudless and bright. A strong and steady breeze whipped the leather skins they wore at their elbows and backs and they stared at an eagle drifting on a thermal like a lone and defiant leaf in autumn. All the world they knew lay spread out at their feet. Mountainside. Forest. Lake.

The girl asked her father if they could see the house, and she followed his sight line to where he pointed out a small patch of white oak shingles on the back pitch of what was the roof, visible against the never-ending cover of green and the thin trail of smoke that rose from the fire in the hearth. Then she turned to look up at the summit, no more than twenty long strides away, its jagged rock bereft of trees and exposed to countless days and nights of sun, snow, wind, and rain. Behind it was only sky, so that in profile the shape of that summit looked to her, too, like the head of a bear staring into the blue. And off to the side, as though on a shoulder of that head, she saw a cairn of rocks, on top of which was perched a large flat stone. She could feel her sweat cool as the wind pushed against her arms and chest, looked over at her father, and pointed to the pile. He nodded and they made those last strides together.

The cairn was wide but no taller than a scrub pine. The flat stone that lay across it looked like a table, the surface smooth and empty of adornment. The girl remained standing at a distance, wondering how her father had lifted the stone and placed it there.

Go ahead, he said. You can touch it.

She walked forward and placed her hands on the marker, feeling for any words or carvings she might not have seen but might yet be present.

Is she just beneath the rocks? the girl asked over her shoulder.

No, said the man. She's buried in the ground below. The remains of her. As far down as I could dig. I wanted nothing to disturb her.

Her hand still floated over the top of the stone.

How did you move this by yourself? she asked.

I don't know, he said. I only remember it was an autumn day when I started, and snowing when I finished and walked back down the mountain with you.

With me?

Yes. On my back. In this same pack.

And it took you that long?

No. Things change that fast.

Tell me, she said.

So they sat down against the cairn of rocks on the side sheltered by the wind, and the man took a deep breath and told the girl that on the morning he woke and found that the woman had died in her sleep, he felt her great struggle had finally lifted and he lay next to her for a long time until he knew what it was he had to do. He took the girl from her crib, gave her water and mashed beets he had cooked the night before, put her in the pack he had made to carry her, and began to gather wood of all sizes, beginning with sticks and limbs, then branches and whole logs from trees he had found fallen in the forest. With these he made an enormous pile on the lakeshore, placing the driest and thinnest on the bottom and the logs and limbs that would make up her bier on top. He stopped only to feed the girl, and it was twilight when he was done. Then he walked back to the house and carried the body of the woman in her blanket down to the beach, placed her at the top of the heap, and set fire to it as the stars were beginning to emerge in the sky.

He remained awake all night, watching the funeral pyre burn, and in the morning rose to feed the girl breakfast, then climbed with her in his pack to the top of the mountain. He placed her in the shade of the ledge shaped like a bear and began to clear a plot of ground of rocks and earth. He wept for the woman and talked to the girl as he worked so that she would know he was still there, telling her how strong and beautiful her mother was but that the time had come for them to say good-bye. And when he had removed as much stone and dug as deep a hole in the earth as he could, he hiked back down the mountain in full moonlight with the girl.

He slept for a few hours, feeling the temperature plummet in the night but having no strength to light a fire. And at sunrise he went down to the lakeshore and gathered up the woman's bones and ashes and wrapped them in the blanket that had covered their bed. Then, with the girl once again in the pack on his back, the man carried the remains of the woman to the top of the mountain that stands alone, laid the bones and ash in the shallow grave, covered it with earth, and piled stones three-deep on top of that earth.

And when I stood up and looked out at the north, he said to the girl, I could see the storm coming. I could smell the snow. It would be summer before I was able to return, and I wasn't even sure then that I wanted to return. I felt a rage. At your mother's death. At my loneliness. At everything in nature. It was then I saw the stone. I had been walking around it for the past two days. I reached down, cradled it in my arms, and howled as I lifted it with all my anger and all my strength. I howled so loud you began to howl with me, and the wind on the mountain was filled with our howling. But I wanted something to hold her memory as well as her remains. And nothing could stop me until I placed that stone right where you see it now.

The girl was silent for a long time, her father silent, too, with his head bowed.

I wish I could remember her, she said finally. Something about her. But I don't.

You were too young, said the man.

Sometimes, though, in my memory, it's not just you and me, the girl said. Sometimes there's another. So close, I can't see a face. But someone is there with me.

The man nodded. I know, he said.

What did she look like? the girl asked.

The man thought for a moment.

You'll see her the next time you look at the surface of the lake, he said.

I want to come visit her every chance we get.

Let's make the climb every year, said the man. On the longest day. The first day we were all together. She would like that.

I would like that, too, said the girl.

Then they rose from where they sat sheltered from the wind and walked back down the mountain.

THE MAN BEGAN TO TEACH THE GIRL WHAT he knew of the lake and the land that summer. He showed her where to dive for the mussels they boiled and served for dinner with a plate of wild onions. He taught her how to make a rabbit snare and a dessert of cattail rhizomes and rose-hip jam for the meal they caught in the snare. He took her step by step through the fashioning of a fishing spear from a sapling split into fours at the top, with the points sharpened and lashed to stone spacers, which she practiced throwing at the fish caught in the weir they had built in the cove on the lake. He taught her how to take sinew from and tan the hides of deer he had shot with a selfbow made of hickory. How to hunt for swarms of wild honeybees when the goldenrod bloomed before the autumn equinox, and how to take honey from the tree where those bees had built their hive. And when they were at rest on the lakeshore in the heat of the day, he taught the girl how to approximate time with the noon mark he had placed on an old and worn erratic come to rest long before on that grassy shore.

WHEN THE NIGHTS WERE CLEAR, HE TOOK HIS daughter outside and taught her how to look at the sky, pointing to the stars along the ecliptic and telling her the names of the constellations that traveled there. In summer she learned to find the hunter Sagittarius, the heart and tail of Scorpius, and the four bright stars of Hercules. In winter, on snowshoes of her own, her father took her onto the frozen lake and pointed out the great Orion, his dog Canis Major, and Sirius, the brightest star in the sky, the one that makes up the dog's nose. And all year long they watched the Big Dipper revolve around Polaris, a star that could be used as a guide, he told her, if she ever found herself uncertain of the way home.

AS SHE GOT OLDER, THE MAN TAUGHT THE GIRL how to read and write in the long evening light of summer and around beeswax candles during winter on nights when there were no stars to be seen in the sky. For a tablet, he used a piece of tin. For a pencil, a charred stick from the fire. When she became adept at writing, he gave her paper bound between leather covers and a graphite pencil, which he kept sharpened with his knife. She asked him once where he had gotten such paper and pencil and he told her only that they had been with him for a long time.

Although she loved the paper and the feel of the pencil between her fingers, in truth, the girl tolerated her writing lessons. Reading was what she loved, and never more than when she was listening to her father read to her. He had books that were his father's, which he handled gently and kept on a wall of shelves in their small house. He read poetry from poets with strange names like Homer and Virgil, Hilda Doolittle and Wendell Berry, poems about gods and men and the wars between them, the beauty of small things, and peace. He read stories true and not true. Stories about a house in the woods, a hunter and a mermaid, and rabbits in search of a home. And when he was finished and had blown out the candle, she would always ask, as though making certain she was back in her own world, These others, they're gone, too?

Yes, he would say. For a long time now.

And we're alone?

Not alone. We have each other. Now go to sleep and I'll see you in the morning.

As she began to study and decipher for herself the words in the books the man read to her, those stories of struggle from long ago came to life again, as though she were hearing them for the first time in her own voice. That was how, without having to leave the peace and quiet of the mountain, she learned so much about what had been and why it had been that way, from tales recounted in old words of an old time on old pieces of paper bound between cracked and fraying covers.

Yet, after she had become a fine reader herself, the girl still asked her father when she was ready for sleep to tell her a story, one he had heard when he was young.

I'm not so old yet, he would say, then think

of something that had surprised him that day, begin with the words, My father once told me about a time, and from there weave a story about a long journey taken, a triumph of great strength, or a treasure lost and found. Sometimes the tales came from the land around the mountain. Sometimes they came from a place far away the man only imagined. Always they ended back in the small house, safe and warm around the hearth fire.

TOWARD THE END OF THE SUMMER IN WHICH THE girl turned seven, when the man had finished following her across the lake in their canoe—for she had become a strong swimmer—and they were resting on the grass, he told her how he and the woman had made the canoe, walking a great distance north to find the white cedar for the ribs, thwarts, and gunwales, then collecting black spruce roots to use as lashings and heating spruce gum to seal the bark seams.

This same canoe? the girl asked, looking again at the boat she had taken back and forth across the lake ever since she could remember.

This same one, he said. It has lasted this long.

And in the fall of that year, the girl and her father watched a bear emerge from the woods and walk toward the lake, splash about in the water until it had a fish in its mouth, then set off back into the forest and up the side of the mountain. The animal reminded her of its profile on the mountaintop, its place next to her mother, and the questions the girl had had when she first climbed the mountain, the most private of which was why, if her mother was so strong, could she not have lived to remain with them. Rather, it was as though she had wandered off like a bear passing through the forest.

Was my mother a bear? she asked out loud when the animal with bluish-black fur and a blaze of white on its chest had disappeared into the trees.

The man laughed and asked, What makes you say that?

She didn't want to stay with us, said the girl. She went away. Up the mountain. Just like that bear.

The man understood then what the girl had been thinking.

That bear would not have stayed even if you had asked, the man said. He looked like a boar to me, with that massive body of his and massive feet. Male bears are content to wander, and so that one was doing what he was meant to do. I was the one who took your mother up the mountain. Remember? She wanted nothing more than to be here with you. But we don't get to choose when we leave here to sleep on the mountain. We all have to sleep on the mountain one day. Even the bear. Even when we struggle with all our will not to.

The man was silent and looked down at the ground for a long time. Then he lifted his head and said to the girl, Come here.

She walked toward him until they were side by side.

Sit down and take off your shoe.

She did, and he asked her to look closely at it. The tanned deerskin. The even stitching. The worn but impenetrable sole.

Your mother made that shoe, he said. When you were still a baby in her belly. She made five pairs of shoes from deer she and I hunted with the bow. Each pair she made is one size bigger, so that by the time you outgrew the last you would be able to make your own.

Is this my last?

Yes, the man said.

How could she have known to make five, asked the girl, if she wasn't sure she would be leaving us?

The man shook his head as if to wonder.

Maybe she did know, he said. And so she thought of a way in which she could stay with you, year after year, right at your feet. Until you were grown enough to understand that we all have to leave.

ONE DAY AT THE EDGE OF AUTUMN WHILE THEY lazed in a hammock the man had strung between two pines, the girl asked if there were any more bears in the forest or just that one they saw in the summer.

There are bears still, said the man. They come and go, but keep to themselves.

I like that the mountaintop looks like one. And that it will always stay right where it is, said the girl.

That's why I put her there, the man said. The bear is a companion to her while she sleeps. I hope one day I'll sleep there, too.

The girl was quiet for a moment, then asked, What are they really like?

Bears?

Yes. Are they nice?

They're shy, the man said, if that's what you mean.

I mean will they roar at us and come eat our food if they're hungry? The real ones?

No, said the man. They don't roar unless you bother them. Or threaten their young. My father once told me they will travel a long way to do good, for their own or another. It's a promise they make when they are very young, whispering it to their mothers even before their eyes are open.

The girl swung slowly in the hammock, wondering what a bear's whispered promise might sound like, until the man asked, Would you like to hear the story my father told me about a bear who saved an entire village by keeping that promise?

Yes, the girl said, and sat up so quickly that the hammock almost overturned them onto the pine-needle floor. The man grabbed hold of the tree just in time, and after a good laugh, he began to tell this story to the girl.

Once upon a time, in a place along a wide and winding river, there lived a king who demanded the villagers in his kingdom give him all of the silver and gold they possessed. They were good farmers on fertile land, but he was the king. So they gave him their silver and gold and went out to their fields to grow the food they would eat, thankful at least for the fruit of their labors. Summer went by peacefully and the villagers were about to take in one of their best harvests ever, when the king demanded they give him all of the grain they had grown.

They resisted, asking, Why would you do this to us? What will we eat? But the king answered none of their questions. He sent his soldiers and took everything the people had harvested, so that they had to live on what they could glean from the dust on the floor.

That winter, not long before the calendar said it was spring, and with the people on the brink of starvation, an old but affable bear came through the village on his way to the fair. When he saw what a state the villagers were in, he asked them why. So they told him.

And after our children die, the village elder said, we will die, and then, of whom will that king be king?

The bear scratched the hair under his hat and asked for a small wagon, a bundle of hay, and a large coat. He put the hay in the wagon, threw the coat over the pile, and set off with the wagon in the direction of the king's palace.

When the bear arrived, he asked for an audience with the king, and when he stood before him, he asked the rich king if he would like to see a dance.

The king said yes, because he was lonely, and so the bear danced.

And when the bear had finished with the performance, the king was so delighted, he asked the bear if he would dance for him again in the morning.

Yes, said the bear. If you give me some food from your stores.

The king agreed, and this was how the bear found out where the king kept the grain he had taken from the villagers. That night the bear filled his wagon and left in the storeroom the hay he had brought.

In the morning, after the bear had danced again for the king, he said that he would come back the next day if the king let him retreat to the other side of the river so that he could practice a new dance. The king agreed, and the bear wheeled his wagon out of the castle grounds, with the grain piled high beneath the cover of the large coat. The palace guards saw the same wagon leaving as the one that had arrived, and so they suspected nothing.

The bear did this from the first quarter moon to the full, leaving only large piles of hay in the king's storehouse. In that time, he gave all of the grain back to the villagers, without so much as the king's cook knowing that it was gone, for he thought the bear had simply eaten his fill and the hay had been there all along.

Now, when the full moon was waning and the villagers could feed themselves again, they asked the bear if he had seen their silver and gold. He said he had, for it was kept in the same row of locked storehouses where the king kept the grain. With their money back, the villagers said, they could raise an army and overthrow the king. And yet, they despaired of ever seeing their fortunes again.

The bear had missed the fair by now and had become fond of the villagers. He scratched his head again and said, I will get your silver and gold back. I ask only that you wait to overthrow your king until I return with my own army to help you.

The villagers couldn't believe their luck.

You have an army? they asked.

Of course, said the bear. It's made up of every animal and tree in the forest.

So the villagers agreed and the bear left for the palace.

The king was overjoyed to see the bear, for he needed cheering up. All of the food he had stored away from the harvest was gone and he didn't know what he could offer.

A piece of silver will do, the bear said, and then I will be on my way.

The king agreed, and the bear danced his best dance ever, after which the king bade the bear to follow his guards to the storeroom and take whatever amount of silver he thought was a fair price for the dance. The bear, true to his word, took one piece of silver and placed it in his pocket. Then he asked if he could sleep there, as it was late and, with the moon on the wane, there would be robbers in the forest.

Now, while the king and all of his court slept, the bear bribed the blacksmith with a silver piece to start his forge, after which the blacksmith could go back to sleep. And when the forge was hot and the blacksmith was snoring away like flabby bellows, the bear melted down all the silver and gold in the storehouse. Then he poured the silver into four molds of four wheels, and the gold into the mold of a wagon.

In the morning the bear took ashes from the forge and blackened the silver wheels and the golden wagon, then wheeled his pile of hay covered with the large overcoat away from the palace, through the forest, and into the village, giving back everything the king had stolen from his subjects in the form of the wagon.

The villagers were beside themselves with joy. They wanted to melt down the silver and gold right away and get to work on their army, when the bear reminded them, Wait for me before you go into battle. Otherwise, it will not go well.

The villagers all agreed. The bear waved good-bye and walked off along the road that led into the forest.

One season went by, then another, and another, and the bear did not return. In time, the villagers went back to their farming, the old king died, and his daughter ascended to the throne. This young woman was intelligent and kind, forgiving and fair. She treated her subjects well, and they worked for her in return. And no one in that village ever again set eyes on the bear.

After the man had finished the story, the girl sat in the hammock, rocking still, and stared off in the direction of the forest.

Have bears ever really talked to people? she asked her father. I don't mean in the stories. I mean when there were people to talk to.

I've never heard one, the man said. The bear we saw was quiet, but maybe he didn't see us, or didn't have anything to say. So I don't know.

He saw us, said the girl.

Well, there's your answer, said the man.

SUMMER TURNED TO AUTUMN. AUTUMN turned to winter. Winter turned to spring. And on the eve of another solstice, the man gave his daughter a brass compass that had been his father's. She learned the cardinal and inter-cardinal points from the sun and stars, and he showed her how to use the mirror and sight to find a bearing. He told her how a long time ago others could travel over and measure land with the precision of a single degree, though this was something he had only read of in a book and did not know for sure if it was true or just a story.

The next morning, as they climbed the mountain that stands alone, the girl held the compass out in front of her on the path that wound around downed trees and diverted across rock ledges, and she could not take her eyes off the needle, which pointed ever north, like an arrow undeflected in its aim.

BY THE TIME SHE WAS NINE, THE GIRL COULD move to the top of the mountain without resting. She would bound from the tree line straight to the summit and stand at the base of it.

Hello, Bear, she would say to the rock formation. It sure was a long winter.

Then she would move back to the edge of the forested path and wait for her father. When he emerged, they would climb the last steps together to the woman's grave and stand in silence with their hands on the flat stone until the sun had moved past noon and they hiked down the mountain once again toward home.

THE YEAR THE GIRL TURNED TEN, HER FATHER gave her a present of a knife with a bone handle and a leather sheath he had made the year he and the woman first lived in the house.

There's more, he said to his daughter.

They walked outside to the man's toolshed, where he kept his axes and saws and instruments for working with wood.

I want to teach you how to make your own bow and arrows, he said. The year we first climbed the mountain together, when you were five, I saw along the way the straightest hickory tree I've ever seen. When I got the chance, I went back and timbered it.

He pointed at the roof of the shed, where four long staves were laid across the rafters.

I got those out of the wood. They've cured long enough. I was just waiting for you to be ready.

The man retrieved the staves and chose the one with the fewest flaws, and over the next several days he began to work the back of the bow with a drawknife down to a single growth ring. He marked the center of the bow for the handle and checked the limbs for bend. Then he cut nocks for the string and tillered the bow until each limb bent evenly. He smoothed the belly and sides with his knife, burnished the wood with a round stone, and oiled the entire surface with deer fat.

He worked slowly but steadily, and each step of the way the man taught the girl how to proceed, letting her have an equal hand in the fashioning of the bow. Two weeks later they strung it with sinew from the backstrap of a deer. The man smiled when he watched the girl draw the bow for the first time and she drew it well.

The next day they went into the woods in search of birch and dogwood for arrows, which they cut and trimmed and fletched with turkey feathers the man had found on the mountain path. Then he showed her how to knap arrowheads made from the bones and antlers of the same deer from which he had taken the sinew, and these he tied to the arrow shafts.

Every day the girl practiced, shooting her arrows into a target of woven hemlock boughs she leaned against a rise. When the man thought she was ready, the two went into the forest and he taught her how to read the landscape, looking for the signs—broken limbs, overturned leaves, traces of blood and scat—that would tell them what animals had been there days or minutes before. If a rabbit had been in search of shelter. If a fox had been in search of food. If each had found what it was looking for. Animals are creatures of habit, he told her, their stories written over and over again. In the snows of winter, or over the dirt ground of summer, there was always a tale playing out, and it was the hunter in the end, if she was a good one, who would write the epilogue.

She brought home squirrel, rabbit, and turkey, and the two of them ate well. The man also gave her a spool of thin line, one end of which she attached to the bow and the other end to an arrow, and the girl taught herself how to shoot fish caught in the weir. Often she missed, but when she hit one and it didn't wriggle off the tip, she came back with trout for dinner.

In the fall, she convinced her father to let her go out alone and stalk her first deer. He was hesitant, but her spirit and her will prevailed. She had watched him dress the deer he had killed year after year, and he showed her how to make a backpack to carry out of the forest any but the largest stag she could bring down. She left with food for two days, and three days later returned, not having fired a single arrow from her bow.

The next year, in the spring, a pair of geese appeared on the lake. The man hadn't seen geese for many years and so thought they were only passing through. But they remained to nest, and by the time of the summer solstice they were a family of seven fowl and had discovered the grassy beach of the cove.

One morning when the girl went down to the lake to fish, she came upon the flock, as surprised to encounter them as they were by her. The mother rounded up the goslings and pushed them into the water, while the larger goose came at her. The girl tried to run but slipped in the mess left on the grass. A sharp blow, as though from a stone, hit the back of her leg and she turned and saw the huge bird towering over her. She put her hands up to cover her head just as it brought its beak down again, striking her in the arm. She pulled in her feet as though to protect herself, then kicked out and hit it square in the chest, stood up, and limped back to the house.

Her father put her in the bath as she sobbed, looked at the wounds on her leg and arm, and wrapped strips of cloth around them when she got out and dried off.

Nothing's broken, he said.

He sat her down at the table, gave her a cup

of tea, and waited for her to regain some of her strength.

After she had stopped heaving and could drink with a steady hand, her father said, They scared you, didn't they?

She nodded.

You scared them, too.

I wasn't trying to hurt them, the girl said, and began to cry again.

The man rocked her in his arms.

You know, they're not going away, he said. So we either let them be and fish elsewhere on the lake until the autumn or you hunt them, just as you did in the fall when you went out for deer.

He pointed to the bow and quiver of arrows in the corner of the kitchen where the girl had leaned them against the wall.

The whole flock? she asked.

First the big one. He's the gander. But if you're fast enough, you can get the goose, too. The fox will take care of the goslings. We could use the meat. And you could use their feathers.

The girl stared at her bow and seemed lost in thought. Then she turned to her father and asked, When?

The man told her there was rain coming that would last a few days.

And you need to give your arm time to heal, he said. When it clears, we'll get up early, go down to the water, and take cover behind the rock. They'll come. When they're out of the water and busy eating grass, you stand and take your shot.

The girl said nothing, thinking only of the ache in her arm and leg and the fear she had felt as the large gander attacked her, fear that was new to her, for it was nothing like being alone in the woods. And yet, it was somehow familiar to her as well, as though it had been there, inside, waiting for a long time.

THEY ROSE EARLY IN THE MORNING ON THE DAY the rains cleared, and she told her father she wanted to go down to the water alone. Dawn sky still gray and the world around her glistening, she sat down behind the big rock with her back to the water and waited.

It wasn't long before she heard the chorus of soft clucking from the goslings as the family of geese paddled along the strand that bent and formed the cove, seven of them swimming in a line, the gander in the front, the goose at the back.

She watched as the gander strutted out of the water and onto the shore. The goslings—bigger somehow than when she had seen them last—followed in line, then broke off, ranging around the beach as they picked at the grass with their beaks. The mother goose was last, cautious as she pecked and watched, wary perhaps of the silence of the morning. The girl nocked her arrow and stood.

The gander was no more than ten yards away. It saw the girl emerge from her cover and squawked at its mate, then raised its head and body to full height, thrust out its wings and neck, and rushed at the girl.

She drew her bow and, in that moment alone there on the beach, wondered what her mother would have done. Wondered with a calm and curiosity so consuming that, had she been able to stop time, she would have walked back to the house and asked her father, Can you tell me what she would have done?

Then the girl released the arrow and sent it

straight through the gander's chest at near point-blank range.

She nocked another and moved toward the water, where the mother goose had opened her wings in one last effort to cover her young, as though to protect them from a danger they would not survive in this world. She drew the arrow and fired in one swift move, hitting the goose square in the back and pinning it to the bottom of the shallows. There she stood and watched as the goslings swam off in four different directions.

THE MAN DRESSED AND COOKED THE GANDER THAT night, and the girl said nothing as they sat down to their supper. The meat was tough and stringy and the man could tell his daughter was only eating what he had given her so as not to be chided.

This is what my father would have called one tough old bird, the man said, trying to get a smile from the girl, but she sat and stared at her plate.

The man pushed his meal away from him.

Tell me, he said.

She took a deep breath and looked up.

It's a jumble of things that won't settle down,

she said. Like in the autumn, when I pull leaves away from the house, and the wind is blowing in a circle, so that the leaves I've removed and new leaves, too, swirl around and settle back where I've just cleared them. I can't get anything clear.

The man nodded.

I've felt that swirl, too. What do you do then? To the leaves? Do you try to push them away faster and farther, so they'll swirl off into the woods? Or do you wait for a day when the wind has died down?

I wait for a day when there is no wind and carry them into the woods, the girl said. Besides, some more will have fallen from the trees by then.

Yes, said the man. So, maybe it's too soon now to clear those leaves from where they're swirling around inside you.

She pushed her plate away, too, and turned her head in the direction of the water.

I've been watching them, though, she said. Two leaves keep coming back. I know I was protecting myself and the water where we get food when I shot them. I don't feel bad about that.

You feel bad about the little ones.

She was trying to protect them.

We could have done it some other way, the man said.

How?

Trapped them. But then we'd still have to kill them, close up, with a knife. And what if, instead of geese, we trapped the loons by mistake?

The girl was silent.

Why am I feeling this? she asked.

Because you're beginning to understand.

Understand what?

That every thing has its end. And we have a part to play, right up to that end.

The girl was quiet again, stared down at the table, then looked up at her father.

You know what I wished most of all? she said. When I was in that bath crying and my arm hurt like a big thumb under a rock?

What? asked the man.

I wished I could have talked to those geese. Told them why we didn't want them making a mess on our beach. Why there were better places to raise their young. Maybe they would have understood. Or maybe they would have taught me something about them. Like that bear who helped the people in the story you told me.

That's what your mother would have done, said the man. Sat down with those geese and said, Now look here. What are we going to do?

They stood and cleared their plates and the man brought mint leaves and hot water to the table. He put the leaves into two cups and poured the water over them and gave one cup to the girl.

Do you want to hear another story? he asked.

No, she said.

It's not meant to cheer you up. It's a story I heard once about someone who understood the animals. It saved him and others like him, when there were others.

Did my mother know it? she asked.

Yes, said the man.

All right then, said the girl.

A long time ago, the man said, long before there were many others who lived on the earth, there were people who lived here, in the shadow of the mountain that stands alone. Except for our books and tools, they lived much the same way we do now, raising vegetables, foraging, fishing on the lake, and hunting in the forest.

One of the men who lived among them was a great hunter they called Thorn. He was revered for his skills with a bow and arrow and his ability to provide food. When he went out to hunt, he would disappear for weeks. It was said that when he began his hunts, he would roam through the forest for two phases of the moon, eating only leaves, tree bark, and insects. Then, for another two phases, he would speak to the animals. Hare, turkey, deer, whatever game he was in search of that season. He would tell them of his respect for their lives, thank them for the example they gave of how to live on the land, and promise them he would plant a field of sweet grasses for their families to eat and share if they would give themselves to his people. Any animal he killed, he dressed quickly and buried the remains, placing on that spot the broken arrow with which he had brought it down.

One long, dry, and hot summer, Thorn came back from a hunt that had lasted a full month, with little more to show for it than a few rabbits and an old buck. The entire forest was at rest in whatever cave or cool patch of grass could be found. Always, when Thorn returned, he left his game with the cooks and smokers, and went into a long, deep sleep.

But this time, after he had been asleep for only a day, he was awakened by the leader of the others.

Thorn! she hollered. Lightning has set the forest ablaze!

Thorn stirred and smelled the smoke sweeping down from the mountain and along the lake. He told them to gather what and who they could and run to the canoes. The island would save them. But when they reached the canoes, they saw that they were already in flames. Not one could be rescued. The fire now backed them away from the shore toward their village, pushing the people farther into the woods. Then Thorn saw a second fire coming down the other side of the mountain. They would all be lost, with nothing left of them but their bones beneath the ashes of the place where they once lived.

What did he do? the girl asked.

Thorn raised his hands and his voice and called upon the power of any animal in the forest that could help him and his people. Any animal who knew him as a great hunter and who understood that he lived as he was allowed and would die the same way, if it were the will of the earth.

They say that Thorn changed then into a

giant puma of silver and brown, put the people on his back, and raced through the burning trees to the lakeshore. There, the puma turned into an eagle the size of a mountaintop and flew the people across the water and brought them to the island. Finally, at the water's edge, there stood the figure of a great bear, who spoke to the tribe in a deep voice. Don't be afraid. Not all is lost, he said, and led them to the highest point of the island, from where they watched the forest burn. And when they turned to thank the bear, all they saw was Thorn standing on the rise that marks the middle of the island, his arms and face raised to the sky as the clouds opened and it began to rain.

Even when she knew her father had finished the story, the girl remained where she sat in the quiet of the evening, fixed on the shadow of the man's face.

What happened to them? In the end, I mean, she said finally.

I'm told the people remained on the island, raising simple crops and fishing. And one day, when he was an old, old man, Thorn took a birch canoe across the lake and walked into the forest, never to be seen again.

The girl turned to gaze out the window. Past her father. Out into the dusk. Out in the direction of the island.

The man rose, lit a lamp, and sat back down.

He said, My father told me and your mother just before he died that the spirit of Thorn lives still on the shores of the lake and along the paths of the forest. He watches over everything here and, for that reason, will never die.

The girl turned back to her father.

Have you ever seen him? she asked.

No, said the man. But I have felt him. When I returned to this house after I had buried your mother, the first night you and I slept here alone, I woke up because I thought I heard the door open in the early morning. It was cold and there was snow and I knew I should put more wood on the fire to keep it alive. But I couldn't move after what I had just done. I can't explain it. I knew someone was there, but I knew, too, that whoever it was meant no harm. Then something like a voice that was not a voice told me to go back to sleep. So I did. And in the morning, the fire was stoked and burning and there was a small puddle of water on the floor that looked like melted snow.

The girl stared down at the fire in the hearth now.

I've felt the same, she said. Out in the forest when I was hunting. Sometimes it felt like someone was with me. Other times it just felt still. Like not a single leaf was swirling. Like everything was where it was supposed to be.

THE NEXT DAY, THE GIRL TOOK THE BLOODSTAINED and unfletched arrows with which she had killed the geese down to the beach, snapped them in two, and drove them into the ground at the base of the rock. Her father had plucked and kept the feathers from the fowl, and from these she took the primaries, searched for new birch limbs to shape, and fashioned two thin, sharp tips from the bird beaks. With these arrows, she spent a day fishing for trout in the sheltered coves on the lake. She knew, because of their lightness, the arrowheads wouldn't last long. But she took five fish home to her father that evening. He salted and dried them and that was their dinner for another week.

S HE TURNED ELEVEN AND HER FATHER GAVE
her a new pair of shoes for a gift. He had
long ago taught her how to make her own and
she did, tanning the hides of deer her father had
killed with his own bow and sewing the shoes
together with the sinew. But the man wanted
these shoes to be especially strong. He worked
on them all winter while the girl was asleep.
When he was finished, the soles were three
pads thick and the insides lined with rabbit fur.
The girl wore them the next morning on their
hike to the top of the mountain, and one year
later they looked no more worn than on the day
she had received them.

AT TWELVE, HER FATHER GAVE HER A SET OF FLINT
and steel in a deerskin bag. And as they stood
at the top of the mountain that morning, over-
looking the forest and lake, he told her they had

to start preparing for a long trip, deciding what they would carry and, though he knew the way, studying the old lands over which they would travel on the map he kept folded in a book.

The girl stood next to her mother's grave and listened, then asked, Where over the lands?

East, the man said, and pointed to where the sun shone, as though it were rising that morning for this purpose alone. To the ocean. After the tanning and the fishing we've been doing, we need more salt. Hickory root isn't enough. Two of our largest gourds full of seawater will give us enough salt to tan a hare's hide.

How do we get it? asked the girl.

We'll take our pots, build fires in the sand, and boil down as much seawater as we can. We should be on the way home again by the autumn equinox.

Is there a path to this ocean?

Not anymore, the man said. My father took me there when I was your age. And your mother and I made the journey twice. On the last, it rained for an entire phase of the moon and we had to shelter in a small cave at the base of a cliff. We lived in there past the equinox, with a small fire to boil water for tea and to cook the fish we caught, telling stories we'd been taught as children. And when the sun finally came out, we dried our things, packed the salt, and walked home before winter set in. You were born on the next summer solstice.

She watched her father as he spoke, watched him stare off into the distance not of sky, but of time, as though searching for the memory of something or someone he had long ago left behind.

What does it look like? she asked. The ocean.

The man breathed in and thought. He could remind her of the poets, but it was some other description she was after. He knew. Some other image she sought.

Do you see the lake down there? he asked. The island, the near shore, the far? All bounded by the forest?

Yes, said the girl.

Imagine if from here everything you saw in front of you—lake, trees, the mountains to the edge of the horizon—was water. Endless blue water of waves in constant motion. That's what the ocean looks like.

The girl frowned.

I can't imagine it, she said.

No, said the man. You can't. Not until you see it. And hear it. And smell it.

The girl remained facing east.

And you said we would sleep on the sand. What did you mean?

There are long stretches of white sand all along where the ocean meets the land, he said, as wide as the distance between the lake and the house. There's always a breeze there and you can smell roses. At night it's like sleeping at the end of the earth.

The girl smiled then, and said, I can't wait to see it with you.

THEY LEFT NOT LONG AFTER THE SOLSTICE. EACH carried a pack. In the man's were the pots, two pannikins, line, fishhooks, bedding, a knife, deerskin pouches for the salt they would bring back, food, and a water gourd. The girl took her own bedding, her comb, a knife, compass, flint and steel, food and water, a quiver of nine arrows, and her bow. When she asked her father why he was leaving his bow, he told her she was enough of a hunter for both of them. And so she shouldered hers alone and they set out.

THEY HIKED NORTHEAST, MAKING A FIRE WHERE they camped each night. It took them from a new moon to the full to travel to the banks of a wide and deep river that meandered in a southerly direction. From that full moon to another crescent new moon, they walked north along the river's western bank, fishing for their food and climbing into the high mountains. So far north had they gone, they sometimes trudged through waist-deep snow in the shaded ravines that held snow all summer, until finally they were able to cross the river in a fast but narrow section of its course, the girl tied to her father with a length of vine, their packs held high above their heads.

Now they climbed down to the south and east and found forests and meadows that held small game, which they hunted, dressed, and cooked. In a grove above a feeder stream that came out of the mountains on its way to the river, the girl shot a young spiker deer with her bow. They remained camped on the banks of that stream and the man butchered the deer and smoked the meat over a rack made with the limbs of trees uprooted and swept aside by spring floods. Then they hiked on.

Another two phases of the moon brought them out of the mountains and foothills and into boglands and shrub swamps on their way east, where tall and lifeless tree stumps fell away when they pushed at them. There were few places there to camp that were not flooded and teeming with insects, and so the man and the girl did not stop to sleep, but kept walking through the night.

SETTING MOON AND RISING SUN WERE BALANCED on the horizon when they crested a hill and came to an expanse of dwarf drumlins and glens rife with rangy grass and flowering weeds that looked like no meadow or lakeside the girl had ever seen, so uniform and unbroken was the landscape in its constant undulation. The man picked handfuls of young pigweed shoots growing out of the ground and placed them in his pack. Then the two of them hiked up a knoll, surveyed the view before them, and sat down to eat. The girl was tired from having walked all night and she wished she could sleep. But her father seemed animated by the place.

He said to her, When I came here with my father, there were still some walls rising out of the ground. Not much of them, but visible. With your mother, more than ten years ago now, there were bricks and glass in the dirt, but nothing standing. Now it looks like this.

The girl stared at the stretch of emptiness.

Walls for what? she asked.

Houses once. Bigger than ours. Row after row of them, if you can imagine. That's all I can do. I've never seen such a thing.

She remained gazing out at the land, then said, The others.

The man nodded.

A long time ago, he said.

For a while the girl just listened to the strange forestlike stillness of the place and began to doze, when she heard the man unshoulder his pack and start walking down off the knoll into a large depression in the ground below them.

She stood up fast and shouted, No!

The man stopped and turned.

What's wrong?

Don't. Don't go. We don't know what's down there.

The man stood midway on the grassy slope.

I don't think there's anything down there to be known, he said. But there may be something we can use.

He continued along the slope of the hill, and the girl watched him as he slowed, walked carefully around the perimeter of a hollow, then disappeared over the side. She stood waiting, trying not to look at the fear in front of her like an oversized gander, when the man climbed out of the hollow and walked back to the top of the knoll.

He held a piece of glass filthy with mud in his hand, and said, This will make a good arrowhead for small game.

He showed it to the girl, then opened his pack, took out a piece of leather, which he wrapped around the glass, and placed it next to the fishing line.

Come on, he said. There might be something else we can find.

The girl hesitated.

The man pointed to where he had found the glass, and said, Just a little farther.

So the girl unshouldered her pack and bow, and they climbed up and down another rise. There the man dug at the dirt to show the girl what the walls looked like. Colorless, flat, and uniform blocks, their hollow cores filled with dirt and insects buried in the loam. He picked up a clod of that dirt and threw it and something moved near the place where it struck. Something small, fast, and of the shadows. He looked at the girl to see if she had seen it, too, but she hadn't and he was glad for it.

They stopped at midday to eat, then searched two more mounds in the afternoon heat but found nothing else, so covered in earth were those remains of what once was, and they moved back to the knoll and camped for the night.

THEY SLEPT FITFULLY ON THE GRASS UNDER THE newly waning moon, two inhabitants of a world recognizable now to no one save those two who had come first, for all the others who had once claimed dominion and name and believed they would be remembered as a result lay inert and buried in the ground.

IN THE MORNING, THEY WERE SOAKED WITH DEW. They made no fire and ate dried venison and pigweed in silence, then packed up what little there was to pack of their bivouac. The sun was just rising out of a haze in the east and the man faced it, knowing they would have to camp two more nights before they reached the ocean, and he turned to tell his daughter this.

He saw it then, the glint of weak light reflected by something on the far edge of grass in a place they had not gone. He walked quickly down the knoll and over to the grass, where he dropped to his knees and began to dig with his hands.

It was another piece of glass, but one in which the man's face reflected back through the dirt and scratches on the surface. He wiped it with his sleeve, returned to the girl, and showed it to her.

What do you see? he asked

She looked into the glass and flinched, then looked again.

It's like looking into the water, but I can see myself so clearly.

Your mother once had a glass like this set in a wood frame with a wood handle. It was her mother's. And someone else's before that.

Is this what she looked like? the girl asked, staring still into the glass.

Yes, said the man.

What happened to it?

I don't know, he said. The last I saw her with it was just before you were born. I never saw it after that.

The girl turned the glass over and over, her reflection the same each time. Then she lowered it.

I'll keep this for arrows, she said, and placed the glass in her pack.

There's an exposed section of wall over there we missed yesterday, the man said. Let's look one more time before we go.

She wanted to say no. She wanted to leave that place behind, keep moving toward the ocean, but her father had always known which way was the best way and why. She took off her pack again but kept her bow and quiver with her and followed him.

The wall that stood on the brow of this hill was little more than four rectangular blocks set in the same course in which they had been set long ago, the exposed and crumbling perpends choked with dirt and weeds, the rest buried. Behind it, though, they discovered a drop the distance of twice the man's height into the old foundation, a dark ravine now cut by years of rainwater running across stone before seeping again into the ground. The sun was rising out of the haze on the horizon, though no light yet illuminated the floor.

That seepage will have uncovered some things, the man said, and eased himself onto the ledge.

The first course of blocks broke away and tumbled into the dark with a splash. The man kicked at the others from where he was crouched. They held and he climbed over the wall until he dangled from his hands, holding on at the top, then let go.

She watched him drop but could see little more than shadows and hear the slosh of water.

There was a long silence and she guessed he was waiting for his eyes to adjust to the dark. All she could see as she peered into the shadows was his head turning back and forth.

It's a mess down here! he hollered.

She expected him to turn then and climb back up the wall and they would be on their way. But she heard him as he began to walk upstream, heard the flinty clang of rusty metal scraps tossed and discarded against what stone lay down there, and as she leaned farther over the ledge, she could see his head start and stop, start and stop. Then his hand would reach for something she couldn't see and didn't even know if he had touched it, and she wondered what could hold him there. What could he be hoping to find?

Then movement that was not the man's. Not the water. Not the weeds that managed to thrive in those shadows and bent now to the arm that grazed them. It was the lift of a tail. She could see it in the slant of light. Only she. And his hand was reaching again. Reaching right into the flash of eyes and teeth.

She shouted the same moment he shouted, stopped, and pulled his hand into his chest, and she reached for her bow and nocked an arrow but saw nothing at which to shoot.

Are you hurt? she yelled down to him.

He lifted his face to the light.

I'm bit!

He backed out of the water and returned to the wall where he had descended, but she knew it was too steep to scale with one hand, so she leaned over as far as she could and lowered her bow. He grabbed hold of the lower limb with his good hand and she pulled him up and over the parapet with a force born of fear so strong, it sent the two of them tumbling onto the grass.

She stood and reached for his hand to look at the bite, but he pulled it back and studied the wound himself. The shape of a mouth and teeth was impressed into the skin on the top of the hand and over a layer of dirt on his palm. He tried to scrape the filth from the bite with his sleeve, but he was shaking and only spread it and stopped.

I need to clean this, he said.

He walked over to the packs, unstoppered a gourd with one hand, and laved the wound palm first, then dorsal side. He stopped and worked a small piece of broken tooth out from under the skin, then poured the rest of the water over the entirety of his hand and shook it dry.

What was it? she asked.

Too dark, he said.

Was it sick, do you think?

I don't know. Angry enough, if it wasn't mad.

THEY CAMPED IN THE SAME SPOT AS THE NIGHT before, boiling water they carried to make tea from the pigweed and using the infusion to soothe the man's wound. They saw and heard no more of any animal that day or night, as though the place never was and never would be ground over which animals of the forest might travel, let alone stay, and the man said he always felt the same when he came through there. Felt the emptiness and silence and didn't know why he hadn't listened to the girl and left right away.

I tried to draw my bow, she said. It was dark, though.

The man shook his head.

No way you could have seen, he said.

AT DAWN, WHEN THEY ROSE, THE MAN'S HAND was swollen and blue, and the girl thought out loud that they should go back home, but the man said the ocean was close and the salt water would be good for cleansing the wound.

We should finish what we came for, he said.

And so they packed up and walked on.

FROM THE MORNING OF THAT DAY TO THE emptying of the light, they moved over a varying landscape of thin woods, exposed rock, and lowland marsh, stopping only to gather yarrow where they could find it, comfrey and broad plantain when they came upon that. Out of these and the charcoal ash from the fire at night they made a poultice for the man's hand, which they covered with plantain leaves and tied tight around the wrist and palm with groundnut vine.

The sun was arcing west in the sky on the third day, when the girl stopped in mid-stride, lifted her nose like a deer in a meadow, and inhaled long and deep. She tried to speak, breathed again, and said, I smell the pine and rose, but there is something else. The smell of—

Ocean, said the man, who was glad for the rest. That's the smell of the ocean.

They wove through the scrub to a bald patch of rocks and stopped at the edge of a cliff. The

wind blew hard and steady and they looked out at
the sea. In the water below, rock stacks emerged
and disappeared in troughs and foaming peaks
of waves that rolled forward, one after another,
growing in size and speed, until they curled and
crashed in a boulder-strewn roar. Beyond that
the surface lifted and fell but seemed never to
move forward, a surface that stretched as far
as a horizon almost indistinguishable from the
water's silvery blue, so that it looked to the girl as
though sea and sky curved up and over to cover
the earth like a dome.

The man scanned the coast, touched the girl
on the shoulder, and pointed in the distance to a
long strand of white.

That's where we're going. Where a creek
comes out, he said.

They backtracked beyond the edge of the hinterland and followed this until they saw sunlight
slanting as it set through a break line in the western clouds, and they turned east again. The girl
wondered at the pain the man must be in, but he
showed no weakness and never slowed from the
path he knew and had walked before, as though
it was this and only this he had to do. They rose

up and over round caps of stone and disappeared again into woods of mixed trees and streams that seemed to appear out of nowhere. The man then hove to the bank of one of these streams as it began to flow downhill, the way getting steeper and steeper, until the course of it tumbled out from the cover of hemlock and beech in a rush and flowed along smoothed and blackened rocks like a long finger stretching seaward into the ebb of waves in the wet sand.

The two stood side by side on the beach, looked out at the water, and listened to the breakers boom against the shore. The girl inhaled the scent and turned to her father.

We should get to the cave, he said before she spoke.

It's close?

Down the coast. Under the cliff where we were standing.

They moved along the beach, climbing over stones that had rolled down from the headland and fording tidal creeks fed by the freshwater from the woods. The sun had long set, a veil of stars thickening the sky, when the man pointed in the direction of the cliff. A tall, round imprint of black looked pressed against a headland wall that rose higher than any of the others along that coast, and they walked toward this as though it were home.

The floor was sand and the back walls were covered in lichen and damp, but the space was large enough to stand in and there was room to spread out those things they carried.

Outside, the girl collected what dried grass, sticks, and driftwood she could find in the dark and brought them into the cave, dug a small pit near the entrance, and used her flint and steel to strike sparks into tinder of shaved cedar, with which she traveled, until the ball smoldered and ignited and there was fire.

THE FRONT CLEARED AND THE NIGHT WAS DRY. The man and the girl sat at the mouth of the cave, sharing what was left of the lake trout and looking in the direction of the waves.

Tomorrow, he said, we'll get our salt fires going.

The wind had settled to a breeze, and when

they finished eating, the girl asked her father how his hand felt.

About how you felt when that goose hit you.

That bad, she said.

The poultice helps.

The girl was quiet for a moment, then said, Why did you go down there?

The man's eyes were on the fire and he didn't lift them to look at her.

It was like a pull, he said. There's so much buried. So much I don't understand. I've always wondered how it all happened.

Your father didn't know?

He knew only your mother's family. And they spoke only of mothers and fathers to their kin.

Did they look for others?

Their whole lives. And when they were done looking, it was just me and your mother.

He stopped and was silent for a long time, the only sound between them the crackling fire and the breaking waves.

So we didn't look anymore, he said finally. We decided to live on the mountain. And wait.

For what? she asked.

For you.

The girl stared down into the fire, too, as though all anyone might search for could be found there, and said, You talk to her, don't you?

The man nodded.

Every day.

She looked up at him again.

I've heard you. You must think you're doing it only in your head or that it's too windy and that I can't hear. But I can.

I know, the man said. There's so much I want to tell her.

What do you tell her?

I tell her about you. Questions you ask, things you've done. How much she would enjoy being with you.

I ask a lot of questions, don't I?

You just did, the man said, and the girl laughed and looked back into the fire.

Did you think you would find her here?

I know where to find her, he said. I just wanted to remember again. Another time I had with her. In this place.

He picked up a handful of sand in his good hand and let it pass through his fingers.

The girl watched him.

Will you tell her something for me?

Anything, he said.

Tell her I have loved learning to do all of the things I know she did, too.

I will, said the man.

WHEN THE GIRL WOKE IN THE MORNING, THE man was bent over the fire, spooning a white ball flecked with dirt and seaweed from a pot. She rubbed her eyes of sleep and watched him.

You should have woken me, she said.

I put a pot on to boil last night after you fell asleep, he said. Plenty of good driftwood I found against the rocks in the moonlight. Have a taste. Our first batch.

His bitten hand was still wrapped in plantain and he held it close to his side. With his good hand, he dropped a pinch of the salt onto the girl's upturned palm.

She licked it.

Strong, she said, and spit a piece of seaweed onto the ground.

The man smiled and shook his head.

We can pick those out when we get home, he

said. Let's build two more fires over there. Above the tide line. Then you can have some breakfast and I'll lie down.

HE WOKE IN THE AFTERNOON AND ROSE SLOWLY. The girl was sitting in the sun, shaping the glass into arrowheads, light glinting as she worked off of the mirrored one. She saw him and put the arrowheads into her pouch. He held his hand close to his side all the time now, as though it had retreated there on its own, and he walked toward the fires.

You slept a long time, she said.

I was tired.

The water boils fast. We'll have more salt by evening.

A few more days, he said, and we should have what we'll need for a while.

She motioned to his hand and said, Let me see it.

He held it out to her. She unwrapped the leaves and peeled off the dried poultice. Teeth marks were still visible in the palm, the skin purple now, the top of his hand a fiery red, with streaks of white emanating from the break.

It's going to look worse before it gets better, he said.

I'll make you a new dressing.

He nodded. Where'd you learn to do the doctoring?

From you, she said.

THEY ATE THE LAST OF THE SMOKED VENISON BY firelight and the girl worried out loud that there wouldn't be food for the journey home.

We can fish, the man said.

Now? she asked.

He watched the line of surf advance and recede on the beach.

Tomorrow morning. On the shoulder of the tide.

She asked him what he meant by the tide and the tide line, and the man told her about the pull of the moon on the earth and the rise and fall of the oceans twice a day, though with time in between called slack, so it was never at the same time every day.

Everywhere? she asked.

Everywhere there's an ocean.

The girl looked at the surf. Why aren't there tides on the lake?

Too small, he said. This ocean we've come to covers almost a quarter of the earth. And that's a large part of the earth. I've not seen it all and don't know if that's even possible, but I've read about it and I believe it's true.

What covers the rest of the earth? she asked.

He staggered to his feet and she rose to stop him, but he said, No. I want you to see this.

He picked up a stick and in the firelight drew a circle in the sand. In the middle of the circle he made an ✕, then told her that if the circle was the earth, only one quarter of the ✕ was land. Water, everywhere from the vernal pools on the tops of mountains down to the bottom of the oceans, covered the rest, and most of that was ocean.

This isn't the only one, she said.

No. When I was a boy, the only other man I met besides my father told us that if you were to walk for three hundred days in the direction of the setting sun, you would come to an even bigger ocean than this one. And there are others.

You believed him? asked the girl.

He came from the west and was on his way back there. We never saw him again.

All right, the girl said. So why does the ocean get a tide and the lake doesn't?

Let me ask you a question, said the man. What happens when there's water in the bottom of the canoe and you rock it?

The water sloshes back and forth.

That's right. So the canoe is like the earth. You are like the moon. And the water in the canoe is the water in the ocean. The water in the lake is just a drop on the gunwhale of the canoe. Alone, it does little. But of all the water in the lake, it has its part.

The girl sat.

The moon does that? she asked.

Every day, the man said.

He looked out across the beach, where waves were reaching so high on shore that sand once dry was now wet and smooth.

The tide's close to high, he said. It'll be low in the early morning, then rising again when we wake. We'll go at the height of that.

The girl nodded. There were many questions

she still wanted to ask, but she left them to the silence now of her father, who sat before the embers of the fire and gazed at them as though they were tiny suns setting on a world of sand and water and he was given this moment alone to see them in the evanescence of their warmth.

HE WAS UP EARLY TO CHECK THE FIRES AND SPOON out another bowl of salt. His neck ached. He looked at his hand and rolled it over in the dawn light. The palm was the color of the horizon, the top a half circle of scabs that oozed pus.

He stood and stared out at the gathering in the east and said, You can't take me from her now. She's not ready. Not yet.

He wrapped his hand with the last of the plantain and a swatch of deerskin and tied those in place with two strips of rawhide. Then he walked over to the girl and nudged her awake.

Tide's just right, he said.

SHE MADE TEA WHILE HE TOOK A HOOK AND LINE from his pack and tied them off. Then he found an arm's-length piece of driftwood and attached this to the line above the hook, about the distance of the girl's height.

The two walked down to the water's edge and the man began to dig with the heel of his foot in the wash, where small bubbles burst up through the sand.

Reach your hands in there like it's a bowl of blueberries and tell me what you feel, he said.

She got down on her knees and put her hands into the slurry, then yanked them out as quickly as she could.

Something bit me! she said.

No, it didn't. That's a mole crab.

He waited for another wave and dug his good hand into the wash and held up a small scurrying crustacean the size of his thumb.

These are what we'll use for bait, he said.

She dug for one more and he ran a large hook through these two, then told her to take off her shoes and put one on her hand. She did, and around this he wound half the fishing line.

Now, here's what you do, he said. Go out into the water about up to your knees and throw that stick as far into the waves as you can. Then pull it in by wrapping it around the shoe on your hand. Fast but not too fast. And make sure the line stays on your shoe. It'll cut you bad.

Her first cast was a long one, and he said, That's it. Now try again and make those crabs look alive.

She did this six times, and after the sixth, she pulled the rig up and onto the beach and left it in the sand.

There aren't any fish out there, she said.

There are always fish out there, he said.

He took the lifeless crabs off the hook and put two fresh ones on.

Now, he said, when you retrieve it, pull the line in slowly, then fast, back and forth, like that.

She waded into the waves and heaved hook, bait, and line as far into the surf as she could.

On her second cast, as she handled the line in the manner the man had instructed her, she felt a great tug, and he saw it.

Pull hard! he yelled.

The line went taut.

Put your right foot behind you and wind that line around the shoe. Nowhere else!

She stood and pulled against the fish and

seemed to shrink in the waves as her right foot sank into the sand. The line was gripping tighter and tighter around her hand and she understood why she had put her shoe on it. After she made a few wraps and the fish broke water with a splash, the man told her to let some of the line out so the fish could run. She felt it dive seaward and worried that she would lose it when it began to slow. Then she felt nothing.

She wound the line in fast again.

It's getting tired, the man said. Keep hauling.

He sat down on the sand.

Keep hauling, he said again in a voice she could not hear. You've won this time.

IT TOOK THE BETTER PART OF THE MORNING, BUT she brought the catch ashore by reeling the line in and backing up slowly out of the sand until an enormous silver-and-black-striped fish flopped and shimmered at her feet in the sun. The man approached it and picked it up by pinching the lower jaw with his good thumb and holding it aloft. The girl had never seen a fish so big.

This will feed you for days, he said, and put

the fish back down, pulled out his knife, and stuck the blade into the fish's head. It made one more lift of its tail, then lay flat on the sand.

FOR TWO DAYS THEY STOKED THEIR FIRES, fished, and slept in their blankets on the sand beneath the stars, the man getting weaker and stiffer in the neck and upper body. On the third, they woke to hissing embers and large raindrops pelting their faces. The girl gathered her bedding and pack and ran into the cave. The man cinched his pack and tried to lift it but could not. The girl ran back onto the sand and took it from him, as though it were no heavier than her bow. He looked wan and weary. She put her hand to his forehead.

You're burning up, she said.

He tried to nod but couldn't. He pointed to the water pots.

Never mind those, she said.

She hooked his good hand around her shoulder and the two hobbled into the cave. She laid him down on the heap of blankets and ran back outside to the pots. She spilled them and wiped them of water and rain, then snapped a stick in two, dug into the ash, and tweezed out the largest coals she could find. She placed them in one pot and covered that with another and ran through the downpour back to the cave.

They kept the firewood they had collected on the dry days in a corner. The girl scooped out the pit in which they had first made a campfire on the night they arrived, placed her coals in it, and covered them with kindling. She blew on the pile until it smoldered and ignited, then stacked on that what sticks and branches she gathered from the floor.

HER FATHER LAY ON THE BLANKETS, SHIVERING and staring up at the ceiling of the cave all day. Every once in a while she sat him up and straightened the bedding as best she could and laid him back down again. She offered him water and he tried to drink but could not, and she pulled the gourd away, dabbed his face with her shirt, and watched him drifting in and out of what sleep he could find.

It was coming on dusk when she realized

neither one of them had had any food since the night before and that she was hungry. Wrapped in salt in her pack was a second fish she had caught, and so she placed seaweed over coals at the edge of the fire and the fish over the seaweed, steaming it and turning it until the meat fell off the bones in great chunks and she pulled it out of the fire.

She asked the man if he was hungry and he gave a small nod.

He sat up and took some fish from the girl and put it in his mouth, tried to swallow, and again could not. He opened his mouth and leaned over, and fish and spit drooled out and onto the sand. He lay back down on the blanket, his eyes wet and wide with crying and what he could not say but what she knew was fear.

By evening, every limb of his body was stiff and spasming, his eyes fixed on the cave wall, his face set in a bizarre rictus that in the firelight belied the pain he was in. The only sound he made was when his body tensed and began to lift off the blanket in a twisted arc and from behind his teeth something that sounded at once like a groan and a shriek passed between those teeth. If she touched him, he flinched. So she sat and talked softly to him, waiting when the spasms came, and starting again when they passed. She reminded him of the gifts he had given her each year on the eve of the solstice, things he had taught her to make, and things she had made with him. She told him his stories would remain with her for as long as she had memory and that if he died, she would take him home to the mountain that stands alone and place him in the grave next to her mother, next to the stone that looked like a bear, and she would live there for as long as the seasons allowed. She said she hoped that would be a long time, for there was one more story yet to tell, the ending of which neither he nor she would ever know.

She woke up with a start in the middle of the night. The fire had died, but there was still a moon in the sky and she could tell he was awake. She put her face over his face and felt his shallow breath, then took his good hand in hers.

His lips moved slowly over his still-locked

teeth, but she couldn't make out what he was saying.

Again. Again, she said, and moved her face so close that his lips brushed her ear.

I'll miss you, he whispered.

She understood now and held his hand tighter.

I'll miss you, too, she said. I'll talk to you. Will you be there to listen if I need you?

Yes, he said.

SHE FELL ASLEEP AGAIN WITH HER HEAD CLOSE to his, listening to the last of those breaths, and when she woke in the morning, the sun rising and bright white on the horizon, he was dead.

She touched his face, strangely softened now after what had taken him had left him, pulled his eyelids down with her fingers, and drew the blanket over his head.

Sleep well, she said.

The rain had ceased. The morning air was humid and still and flies from inland had begun to swarm without the ocean breeze to keep them back in the marsh and hinterland. It was at least another moon to the equinox, she realized, and two more until she could be home. She turned to face the sea and walked out of the cave, sat down in the sand where the fires had been, and wept.

SHE DID NOT MOVE OR EAT OR EVEN DRINK FOR ALL of that day and into the next. When she slept, she slept heeled over on the sand. When she woke, she rose and sat in the same position, staring out at the sun rising another day like it had the day before and would do so on the morrow. A breeze from the west picked up in the night and blew strong enough to take off the tops of breakers as they crashed onshore, and with that breeze came the humus smell of forest and creek water, and the girl knew in her hunger and her grief what she had to do.

SHE ROSE TO HER FEET AND TRACED A CIRCLE IN the sand with the radius of her own body, then with her bare hands dug it out to the depth of her forearm and lined the bottom of it with the flattest rocks she could find. Much of the surrounding land was still wet from the rain, so she took all of the logs that were left in the cave and stacked them in squares in the pit. Then she went in search of more wood from the forest.

All day she pulled limbs of deadfall from along the creek and ranged farther north in search of driftwood. By the afternoon, a heap of small tinder, long branches, and dead logs lay drying on the beach in the sun. And as that sun set behind the western headland above her, she built the pyre in the sand for the man.

The moon would rise late, she knew, but she did not care to have any light save the light from the flames. For a bier she used his blanket and pulled the body from the cave onto the beach until she reached the pit, then gathered man and blanket in her arms, lifted him with one loud howl of anger and rage for her loneliness in the world, and placed him on the coppice she had gathered to receive him.

She took all of the cedar shavings she had left in her pack, bark from the wood she had gathered, and the paper maps her father had carried and consulted on their way, and struck her steel to flint until that bundle of tinder caught fire from those sparks and began smoking in a tiny corner of the pyre. She blew with what breath she had, so weak was she from hunger and exhaustion, but it was enough for the flame to rise and catch and spread along the bottom of the heap. And when the blaze was all-consuming, she went back to the cave one last time, picked up her bow and arrows, and returned to the fire. She balked from the heat as she approached, lifted the bow and deerskin quiver above her head, and threw them into the middle of the conflagration. Then she sat back on her knees, covered her face in her hands, and fell forward in the sand like some prostrate pilgrim of old, unable or unwilling in her humility to watch as the fire rose higher and higher to claim the man.

S*HE WAS ALONE IN THE CANOE, PADDLING TO shore, where her father waited for her, but the lake was so vast that it seemed endless as her prow cut through the water and time slowed and the leaves of the trees on the island began to change from green to yellow and red. She smelled overripe blueberries and wanted to dip her hands into the water and press them against her face, but the wet she felt on her face was warm and thick and smelled of fish.*

THE BEAR ROLLED THE GIRL OVER WITH ITS SNOUT and licked the crusted sleep and salt from her eyes, and she woke staring at a blurred and head-shaped eclipse of the sky.

Are we home? she asked where she lay huddled and shivering in the sand.

No, said the bear.

The girl shook herself and tried to stand in one move and collapsed.

The bear stepped back and the two watched each other from the distance between them.

Can you make another fire? the bear asked.

The girl didn't answer. She thought to run, retreat crabwise up the beach and make a dash for the rocks. But a weakness and thirst beyond any she had known before began to stab at her. She had no idea how long it had been since she had had food or water. No idea how long she had been asleep. She looked at the blackened sand that had once been a fire an arm's reach away from her and no smoke rose from the pyre. No embers smoldered. No heat remained.

Smaller this time, said the bear.

She turned back to look at the animal and remembered the bear she and her father had seen fishing years ago on the lakeshore, the blue-black of its fur, the white mark on its chest, traveling alone. This one looked the same. Male bears wander, the man had said, and it was best to let them. For one fleeting moment, she reached for her bow but pulled back her hand before it even touched the sand.

There's nothing left to burn, the girl said.

There's always something left, said the bear,

his voice sounding like the roll of distant thunder long after a storm, though deeper somehow, as though with that distance there came a present sadness equal to her own.

Look over there.

She turned toward the headland and saw a pile of brush and limbs on the beach.

I collected it while you were sleeping. You need to eat if we're going to leave here.

SHE REGAINED SOME STRENGTH WITH A HANDFUL of unripe rose hips she seeded and dehaired and ate between gulps of water she took from the creek. With dried beach grass and birch bark, she raised a small fire and fed it with the brush and tree limbs the bear had gathered. Then she took a trout the bear had caught for her in the brook that ran through the forest, wiped it and gutted it, and cooked the fish on green switches and wet seaweed over coals she pulled to the side of the fire.

She ate with a ravenousness that let nothing go. When the trout was no more than a skeleton with its eyes sucked out, she looked up for more and realized she hadn't seen the bear in a while and wondered if he might not have been some trick of the mind or apparition. But that wouldn't explain the fish, she thought, and saw the bear walking on all fours down the beach toward her, two more fish in its mouth. When it came close to her, it dropped one on the sand. She eyed the fish the bear still had in its mouth and he flipped it at her so that it nearly landed in her lap. She picked it up and sliced it open with a swipe of her knife, pulled out the guts, and cooked it on the same grate of green sticks in the fire over which she had cooked the other.

EVENING FOUND THEM SITTING BEFORE A BLAZE heaped with deadfall burning like a small beacon that might once have been a signal to ships in search of safe harbor but burned now for ships no more. The girl sat again at a distance from the bear and would not say a word, so consuming was her suspicion, her fear, her grief, and this the bear seemed to understand. He shuffled his bulky frame on the sand and told the girl that all of the forest had believed the pyre on which she had set her companion was a wildfire sparked by lightning in the late summer, which they often were, and every living thing began to move to what protection it could find when the ash and smoke were on the wind. But the eagle, who could see these things, told the bear of the girl and he alone walked to the coast and found her asleep. He had seen her before on the shores of the lake and marveled at her as she fished with her bow, so that when he saw her here, lost and without her companion, he knew it was he who would make the journey with her back to the mountain that stands alone.

She remained silent as he told her this, and she was silent still for a long time when he was done, until she looked at him through the fire and said in a sullen tone, He wasn't my companion. He was my father.

I know, said the bear. And I'm sorry.

And how is it you can speak to me? asked the girl, grief and anger both at the edge of her voice.

There will be a time and place to answer that question, said the bear. This is neither. It's already past the equinox and we need to be on our way if you are to make it home before winter.

I slept only a day, the girl said.

You slept through a moon, said the bear.

The girl watched the dance of shadow and flame on the snout of the bear as he spoke, then looked out at the night sky, where a moon approaching full was just breaking the horizon.

That will be the harvest moon in a few days, the bear said. I'll tell you I fear our time is already past, but we will go as far as we can and do what we need to do.

The girl looked back at the fire and then to the bear.

Why did you wait that long before you woke me? she asked.

Because sleep is the only balm I know, said the bear.

She lay awake on her bedding in the cave throughout the night, until she drifted off into a half sleep toward dawn, then woke with the sun, reached for her bow again, and found only the cave floor. She rose and did not start a fire. She opened her father's pack made so long ago from the skin of a deer and emptied it of salt, knife, pans, fish line and hooks, and walked out onto the beach, where the bear was sitting and staring at the eastern horizon. He turned and watched the girl as she took off her shoes and, holding the empty pack, stepped barefoot into the heap of ash that was once the fire on which she had laid the man, watched as she kicked at the blackened logs gone cold and began walking in a gradually tightening circle that tended toward the center, then stopped and knelt down.

For a long time she remained on her knees, her hands by her sides, her eyes on the ground. Then she raised her head and began to pick the bones of the man from the ashes and the blackened sand, their size and lightness catching her as she lifted and held each one for a moment of longing before sliding it gently into the tanned skin. Arm bones. Legs. The back and pelvis. Neck and clavicle. She brushed aside a mound of charcoal to find the skull and she held this remnant in her hands and gazed at the empty eyes and nose, the teeth pearled like nacre from the fire, the top of the head cracked and smeared with ash. She pulled it close against her chest and cradled it, and again she wept.

When her fingers, blackened and cut, had searched for all the remains she could find, she stood and began to scoop what soot-clogged sand had laid around the skeleton and poured this gently from her hands onto the bones in the skin, so that she appeared to be kneeling in a circle of white in the middle of the surrounding ashes. Then she walked out of the pit and back to the cave. There she rolled up the skin holding the bones like she would have any length of bedding, bound it with two lengths of rawhide, and tucked it deep in the bottom of her own pack. On top of it she placed the things her father had carried and one pouch of salt. And on top of these she put her knife, compass, purse of flint, steel, comb, and glass shards, and what food she had left that would travel. She hoisted the pack and shouldered it and walked down the beach to tell the bear it was time.

THEY SET OUT AT ONCE AND FOLLOWED THE creek into the forest, then walked north-northwest by the points of the girl's compass, back through the hinterlands and dense pine forest, the bear either indifferent or in awe of the wayfinder the girl held and followed unswervingly, though she could not tell. They camped the first night on an old and bald tor under the moon that backlit the distant coast and shone on the foothills to the west, and in the morning rose and walked on.

IT WAS MIDDAY, THE LAND DOTTED WITH BIRCH stands and patches of ground cedar, when the bear stopped the girl and asked what she was holding. She told him it was a gift her father had given her, one that pointed ever north no matter how or where she held it, and the bear said, Then hold it out in front of you now. We need to go north from here.

The girl did not question him, and for the rest of that day until sunset the two walked without stopping and lay down without a fire in a pine forest that whispered around them all night. And when they set out again in the morning and climbed to the top of the highest hill they had climbed since leaving the coast, the girl realized that the way the bear had taken her skirted the place of the walls. She wondered if he knew what had happened there, or if he avoided those lands as a matter of instinct and course, but she did not ask him, and she did not look back from the top of that hill for a glimpse on the horizon of those lands.

THE DAYS THAT FOLLOWED WERE DAYS OF WARM sun and fresh breezes in the forests, and the two rose early each morning to gain time. They traveled north one day, due west the next, and northwest on a third, one always taking the lead from the other as they set out with the sunrise, so that, though they seemed content with their progress, their way resembled more the path of lost and superstitious rovers, the two wandering

upward against escarpments and around valleys, looking not as though they followed the
wildness of the terrain but as though a die were
cast each night before they went to sleep and it
was chance that shaped the direction in which
they would set out come dawn.

THEY ATE TROUT THE BEAR CAUGHT IN THE
freestone streams along which they camped, pine
nuts the girl shredded like a squirrel from the
cones, and wild grapes and raspberries they found
in great autumn bunches, which the bear siphoned
off the vines and branches as if they were no more
than air. They ate mullein, rose hips, and cattails.
As they journeyed farther, they gathered hickory
nuts, sassafras, the samaras of maple trees, and the
inner cambium bark of the birch and white pine
when they began climbing deep into the woods.
The bear seemed to know where every fruit, wild
plant, and nut-bearing tree lay on or close to their
path, and for this the girl was as surprised as she
was grateful for the food of the forest.

ONE MORNING, THEY FOUND A PATCH OF goldenrod in a meadow, blooming like the sun, and the bear stopped and watched as bees drifted from flower to flower, then flew off with their lading of pollen. Each one he followed with his snout and stared in the distance after them, as if content with observing their labor alone, until he said to the girl, This way.

They strode in a straight line from the meadow into the forest and came upon a great lightning-struck maple split and broken off in the middle, bees ferrying in and out of the stump, the low hum of their presence just audible above the ground. The girl knew then what they were after. The bear had watched the bee-line from the flowers back to the hive, just as her father had in days gone by, and he had found the honey tree. Without a break in his stride, he shimmied up the trunk until he was even with the split and reached his claws and face into the hollow. Worker bees swarmed him and covered his snout, but it seemed to faze him not at all. The girl watched from below as he held on to the stump with his back feet, digging with the other two into what lay inside, and consuming by the clawful bees, larvae, waxen comb, anything that clung to the fur of his toes.

THERE WAS LITTLE TALK BETWEEN THEM AS THEY walked in the direction of the high mountains day after day. Their language was the steadiness of gait and the gathering of food.

It was almost noon when they came to a small grove of three walnut trees at the top of a hill in a field where no field should have been, and the bear set off alone into the field, heading in the direction of the trees. When he realized the girl was not with him, he turned, saw her waiting in the trees, and called out in his thunderous voice, Are you coming with me?

The girl stepped into the clearing.

My father taught me to wait when I came to the edge of a field, she hollered back to him.

Your father taught you well, the bear said, and continued at a trot up the hill.

The girl watched, then stepped into clumps of bluestem turning coppery in the autumn chill. The only other time she had been in a field so open was when she and her father had gone on a deer hunt in the autumn of her tenth year. She was learning to track, and they ranged far from home before they saw any game, and when they did, the buck her father shot with his bow bounded from the woods into a field much like the one before her now, lay down in the tall grass, and never rose. She had wanted to run right to it, but the man held her back and spoke of the difference between the hunted and the hunter, fear and calm, blindness and sight. When the man was sure the buck had bled out, they went in search of it and found it in the grass, dressed it, and carried it home. She thought of her father now, his trust in her as a hunter, the death of the man neither hunting nor hunted, and she missed him with a sadness that matched her fatigue. She breathed in to steady herself, smelled the leafrot smell of autumn, and felt the deepening chill in the wind that bent back the grass scratching her knees. Winter was not far behind and she was hungry. She did not know what would ever assuage her grief, but food would assuage her hunger. So she shifted the pack on her back and continued on up the hill toward the bear.

There in the small grove, walnuts hung in bunches of green from the outer branches of the trees. Husks broken open and brown lay on the ground, their meat scavenged by birds and squirrels. The bear rubbed his body against the biggest of the trees, stood up on his hind legs, and began to shake the first branch he could reach. Walnuts rained from the limbs. He stood down, moved to the other side of the tree, and did this to another branch. More nuts dropped like hail in a storm. He moved on to the next and did the same to all three trees on that hill.

The girl didn't have to be told. She took the woolen wrap from out of her pack, spread it out on the ground, and began to collect the nuts that had fallen. And after they had eaten their fill and the girl had wiped her blackened fingers in the grass, the bear finished licking his claws and said, There's an apple tree yet. I can smell it.

They walked up and over the other side of the hill in the direction of where the forest began again, and at the opposite edge, growing in the verge of sunlight and shade, stood an apple tree, not large and not completely full, but big enough to hold more apples than the squirrels and deer could eat. The bear approached, stood, and shook this tree, too, so that fruit dropped to the ground and the girl gathered what had fallen. Some of the apples they ate where they lay. Others the girl tied in her wrap and placed in her pack. By the time they were done, the sun had arced past its midpoint in the sky, and the bear stretched his head and body into the air.

Are you ready? he asked the girl.

She nodded and the two walked into the forest as though on a path already marked and trod.

THE MOUNTAIN RANGE TOWERED SNOWCAPPED and dusk-lit to the north when they emerged from the forest and stopped at the river. They could hear the rumble of the course for some time as they came through the woods, and now the roar of the current before them was so loud that they retreated back to the edge of the trees to make their camp.

The bear fished in an eddy from the river-bank and the girl raised a cookfire. Around the fire, after they had finished eating, the girl told the bear she and her father had walked along this same stretch when they came out of the high mountains, where they had to go in order to cross the river from west to east. Even in the middle of summer, her father had tied her to him, so strong was the current, and still she thought she would be swept away. The bear said it was a swift river and that he had seen a cub drown wading into it not far from where they now sat. They,

119

too, would climb into the mountains ahead of them, he told her, but the high peaks were far off yet, too far to reach before winter at their pace. Tomorrow they would go due north and, if it didn't snow, in a few days they would reach a cave where they could both shelter.

So I won't get home, the girl said, not a question but the same flat, indifferent tone she had been using with the bear.

Not on this side of the solstice, he said to her. Not with this river in front of us and this much cold in the air.

We can follow the river until we come to the snows and I can cross on my own, the girl said.

Cross now where you could not cross before? the bear asked, and he pointed with his snout at the distant range, the sunset reflected in its alpenglow.

Already it's begun, he said. We'll climb until we come to the tree line. And then we both have to prepare.

THE EVENING WAS COLDER THAN THE ONE BEFORE and the girl built up the fire with the abundance of deadfall that lay all around, and with the river a short distance from the stand of beech in which they sat, its rushing current sounded to her like a chorus of more voices than she had ever heard, and she asked the bear again how it was he could speak.

The bear shifted and sighed and was quiet for a time. When he spoke finally, he said that long ago all the animals knew how to make the sounds the girl and her father used between them. But it was the others like her who stopped listening, and so the skill was lost. As for the bear, he learned it from his mother, who learned it from her mother. Not all animals had the range of voice that could be heard, he said, but all living things spoke, and perhaps the real question was how she could understand him.

The girl sipped at her tin cup of pine-needle tea and considered the question, then said she found it hard to believe that all living things needed to speak.

Believe, said the bear. Whether you hear them or not, they need it like they need air to breathe.

The girl had found a place to sit by the fire in an old and gnarled system of tree roots that grew out of the ground like a wizened hand. She looked down at them in the firelight and followed them with her own hands as she fell deeper into thought, studying the way the beech roots formed a series of knuckles and fingers that branched from the thick silvery trunk and disappeared into the ground.

What about trees? she asked.

Trees, too, said the bear, and glanced up in the dark at the tops of those same beech limbs. The trees are the great and true keepers of the forest, he said, and have been since the beginning. Some animals of old have said it was the trees themselves that taught them to speak, for they never make an unnecessary sound. Each word, like a breath, carries with it some good, some purpose. For this reason, trees are the wisest and most compassionate creatures in the woods. They will do all in their power to take care of everyone and everything beneath them, when they have the power to do it.

The girl's doubt had turned to wonder now, and she leaned forward in the firelight and asked the bear, What do they sound like when they speak? It's not like the sound of rustling leaves, is it?

The bear, too, now thought for a moment, and said, Go down to the riverbank. There is a stone there around which the floods have passed for so long that a deep eddy has been dug on the downstream side. That's where I've been catching my fish. Go and listen.

The girl stood and walked away from bear and beech along the bank to the water's edge, where she found the stone and the hole and bent her ear toward the water that eddied slowly around the stone. She heard the sound of a gurgle and a hiss all at once, slower than the rest of the river rushing by, for the water seemed pulled back by the depth of the cut. She put her hand into the current as though to touch the sound, then pulled it out, walked back to the bear, and sat down.

The bear knew both what she had heard and not heard, and while she sat in silence now, he told her that the voices of the trees were the voice of the forest, and that when they spoke, they spoke with such indifference to time that it would take the girl several moons to hear one of their conversations, the better part of one just to hear a single word. But to them it was no different from any story told to any other around a fire in the night, a word spoken in a moment, or a lifetime.

Did you never feel as though the trees around you on your mountain were somehow companions to you and your father? asked the bear.

Yes, said the girl, and thought back to when she was younger and would sit alone in the forest on a blanket of moss and listen to the wind. There were times when she believed she heard a voice that was not the wind, a voice as old and slow and gentle as water curling around stone.

Those were the trees, replied the bear, companions to us all who forget nothing that happens in the forest beneath them and whose memories span seasons beyond count. For each one carries the memory inside of every living thing that has ever touched it or passed beneath the shade of its limbs and leaves, trunk and branches. Every living thing that has ever walked the earth.

The bear looked into the fire then and said, The wood you burn to cook your food and keep you warm? The smoke that rises was once a memory. The ashes all that is left of the story it belonged to. Why else would you be carrying the ashes of your father?

The two were quiet then for a long time, until the girl put her hand on the pack she always had next to her and said, So they will remember us, won't they?

For as long as they stand in the forest. Of that I am certain.

THE GIRL AND THE BEAR SAID NOTHING MORE that evening. She built up the fire with what little wood remained and wrapped herself in her woolen blanket, for she knew by the clear sky that there would be frost that night. And as she lay staring up at the sky, feeling the warmth between fire and forest diminish, she picked up her blanket and crossed through what was left of the ember light to lie down for the first time since they had set out on their journey near the warm belly of the sleeping bear.

THEY CLIMBED NOW ALONG THE THIN marking of trail, such as it was, in a single file that bunched up and stretched out as the bear followed the scent of late-fall berries and the girl went with her knife in pursuit of a lone squirrel foraging acorns beneath leaf fall. Then the trail widened and the two fell in close again and walked side by side along a feeder stream that found its way to the river they had left below.

The bear meant for nothing more than to pass the time when he asked the girl to tell him more about her father, and so she spoke of the man's skills as a bowyer, how beautiful and balanced was the hickory bow with which she had watched him hunt, the arrows of birch he made, arrows that never missed their marks, with tips so sharp that they touched blood before they ever touched dirt. And the bow he made with her, the day he showed her the staves out of which he fashioned it, the carving and the tillering and the care he took to make it a bow she would have a long time, to feed her and protect her, though protection was never something she thought she would need in the forest, until they came to the place of the walls. That was why she had burned it on the pyre with the man's body, so blind with grief and rage was she for not having killed first the animal that killed her father and believing she no longer deserved what had been given to her and so it should go back to its maker, leaving her to fend for herself and die if that was what it came to.

The bear listened quietly as they walked along, listened to the words that started out as praise for a maker, then turned to smoke drifting up and away, as though released from some censer after the worshippers who swung it long ago had themselves become ghosts. And when the girl had finished and the sounds of their footsteps were all that filled the silence, the bear said to her, You speak as though they are gone, but you are still carrying both the man and the bow, as you should. Look around you, though. By your own account, you can fashion again whatever you need to survive. He saw to that long before he died.

The girl said nothing, only nodded her assent to the words of the bear and continued up the spine of the stream and its waters, which ran faster and narrower down the mountain.

AT DUSK THEY ARRIVED AT A ROCKY HOLLOW where the stream rushed loud and unrelenting through bowlegged roots of trees and over the stones of a large waterfall that dropped into a deep pool. They ate small brook trout the girl caught with the hook and line she had taken from her father's pack, fish so small that the hook made them difficult to catch and she was lucky to have landed two. After this supper, the bear went in search of ants and grubs he would rake from the rotting underside of wet and blown-down logs scattered along the steep bank, while the girl remained sitting before the fire.

When the bear returned, he sat across from the girl and seemed to sway in the firelight. He told her he was beginning to feel the need to sleep overcoming his need to eat, and even his voice sounded deeper and more distant now. The cave he knew was yet another day's hike into the range. It was a good cave and would serve her well for the winter, he said, but she should know that the day was coming soon when she would be alone again.

The bear said nothing else, and they sat in their silent companionship around the fire and felt its warmth. Above them, clouds skittered away, revealing the stars of a cold and moonless night sky. But the girl's gaze remained on the roar of the fire she had raised to last the night, and she felt glad for the heat of it on her face.

The bear said from the shadows, You miss him, don't you?

The girl said nothing in reply and the bear sat up on his haunches and continued to sway in the firelight.

More than this will remind you of him, he said. And you will feel the loss like cold closing in around you. I know.

You don't know! said the girl in a loud and sudden voice. Every morning I wake, I expect to see him. Every time we round a bend. Every snap of stick in this forest is one that he is breaking just ahead of me. And in the evening I'll see a shape out of the corner of my eye, but when I look, it's just the flames or the moonlight. And I wish it wasn't.

I do know, said the bear again.

You don't! shouted the girl.

The bear tilted his head back and pointed to a cluster of stars low in the sky, and with the same deep and rolling voice said, Look. That is my ancestor. The Great Bear. Do you see her? My mother taught me how to find her and use her as a guide.

I see it, the girl said. My father taught me to follow the dipper that points to the North Star, just like the compass he gave me.

Yes, said the bear. But look in the other direction and you see not just the tail but the body entire, abandoned there in the forest of night.

His outstretched claw then traced across and to the left corner of the sky, as though he were drawing the constellation itself into existence.

No matter how far and wide I wander through the woods or in my sleep, I look up and take my bearings from it, just as I was taught.

The fire cracked and settled into flames of orange and blue that leapt around the logs like ants the bear pursued.

That's why you're alone, the girl said.

Until this autumn, yes, said the bear. Wandering now with you. But I miss whom I once could touch, as all must do when we make our way through whatever forest or wood it is in which we travel or are raised. This does not mean the man is lost or has disappeared forever. For although he no longer walks beside you, he still remains in the time and place of memory and this is where he will appear again and again, as often as you will seek him. Not only in those places where he has always been but where he could not be then yet will be now. In the slant of light on a lakeshore. In the silence between footfalls along a path. In the scent of wood smoke from a fire around which you will sit alone. Have you not come to know something of your own mother in the stories your father told, the places she walked, the tasks she learned, which she knew her mother knew well?

Yes, said the girl.

This is what I've been trying to tell you, said the bear. Your father knew this, too. What he didn't understand was that you never knew what it was like to miss your mother in the way he missed her. Now you do. Once upon a time, loss was, for many of your own, the only constant they knew. But it is no less difficult or constant now that it is only you. Nor will it be on the day the earth alone misses you, though it will see years of my own cubs born and sent to wander before you cease to rise with the sun.

THEY WOKE IN THE MORNING AND SHOOK OFF the cold and rose to go. The girl emptied what water was left in her gourd. The bear licked at dew on the ground as he moved his head up and down, as though giving a slow and solemn nod. Then the girl gathered her pack and the two set out due north until the stream became a trickle of groundwater and then flowed not at all as it retreated into the rock and moss and dirt from which it had sprung.

They journeyed two more days along this mountainside, stopping only to sleep and to gather food from the inner bark of white birch and the red cones of a staghorn sumac, the drupe from which they ate in bunches along the way. And as they emerged at the tree line after a long climb on the second day, the light failing in the east, the bear took a turn onto a steep path that switched back and forth up a ladder of stones. He took each one by leaps and bounds despite patches of lichen and fresh snow, and the girl struggled to keep up without falling. The last of the sun's rays disappeared into the west and the girl was certain she could go no farther in the dark, when the bear stopped on a shelf of rock and scrub, then pressed on, so that it looked as though he had passed through a stone wall and disappeared into the mountain itself. The large crevice looked like nothing more than the shadow of rock on rock, next to which grew two stunted white cedar trees like tiny sentries guarding a fortress. The girl stood on the ledge and nearly shouted for the bear to come back, when he walked out of the crevice and motioned with his head for her to follow, and she passed through it and into the mountain.

The cave was large enough for the girl to stand up straight inside and still put her hand between the ceiling and her head. It smelled of moldy straw and the damp of a root cellar. She let her eyes adjust to the dark, then began to gather dried pine twigs, leaves, and brown cedar boughs from the corners of the cave and built a fire near the mouth of it. The bear told her she would struggle to keep it going long because there would not be much hardwood this high up, but she went out in search of what she could find to burn and returned with deadfalls of white birch branches, dried cedar, and sticks of maple, which she piled onto the tinder. It smoked more than it burned, the cedar sap popping and hissing in the flames, but it cast light and the girl could see that the cave had been well used over the years by what animals might have found it a convenient resting place. Mice and red squirrels had piled acorns. Snakes had shed skins. Bats had left their black and desiccated guano on the floor. Another waypoint from which any that entered would rise in the morning and journey on.

The bear seemed neither to notice nor to care about the condition of the cave. He walked in slow circles around the inner sanctum, as though he had lost something and was looking for it. Then he lay down against the back wall and asked the girl in a slow and quavering voice, How is your fire going?

I've made warmer ones, she said.

Snow and cold are coming, murmured the bear, and made a noise that sounded like a snuffle. Remember the fire.

I'll keep it going, said the girl.

Until spring. Don't go from me, he said, as though each word were a breath. As though pleading.

Don't, he said again, and was asleep.

The girl tended her fire until it was nearly burned down, then told the bear she was going out to look for more wood and that she would use the glow from the entrance as a beacon for her return. She pulled her blanket tight around her for a wrap and walked out into the dark, where she found a dead white pine not far from the cave, pushed it over, and dragged it back, laying one section of the trunk over the fire at a time, and fell asleep, too, on the closest thing that had come to a hearthstone since she had left her house near the mountain that stands alone.

SHE WOKE COLD. THE SKIES HAD CLEARED OF a front that had passed in the night and the air was icy and still. She stamped her feet for warmth, placed some dried leaves over coals she had banked in the night, and blew on them until a flame rose. It was strange to her that the bear was not up before she was. When she had a stack of kindling burning well, she walked to the back of the cave and tried to wake him.

She approached slowly, but when she touched his shoulder and whispered to him, the bear slept on.

She stood back and looked at the mass of black curled in a ball, rising and falling in the dim firelight of the cave, then knelt down to study his face. The head was burrowed in the front paws resting on the stone floor and pulled around to touch the back feet like the closed loop of an improbable snare. She listened to his breath as it snuffled gently in and out and knew that even if she stood up in the cave and shouted at the top of her lungs, the bear would sleep on. She was alone now.

She made sassafras tea, tended the fire, and looked out on the surrounding forest, a mottle of snow and stone and fallen leaves. Scrub pine and white cedar grew from out of wide cracks in the mountain. Beech, maple, and a few stands of birch rose in the distance below the tree line. She could live for a time on nuts, samaras, and the bark of the birch and pine. She had seen and gathered nuts from a hickory that was half a day's walk down the mountain and she knew there were still some to be gleaned from the branches and forest floor. This wouldn't take her through the winter, though.

All that day she collected firewood to burn, foraged for pine nuts and bark, and found a seep from a rock, where she filled her gourd with water. By the evening, the sun had set behind a sharp bank of clouds and the air had the heavy cold-moisture smell to it that she knew presaged a storm. She built up the outer wall of her firepit with stones to block the wind and direct the heat, drew the coals in close, and placed two big logs on them. After she had some of what she had foraged for her supper, she went to sleep wrapped in her woolen cover, the wind on the mountain rising to the pitch of a howl.

THE STORM CAME BEFORE DAWN, SNOW DRIFTING around the mouth of the cave, the forest invisible except for the black lines of trees that appeared and disappeared with the ferocity of the wind. It lasted the entire day and into the next. The girl went through her meager rations and in the morning, when the snow let up and the winds died down, she went outside to forage again.

THE SUN SHONE NOW BETWEEN CLOUDS BREAKING up and moving fast across the sky. Snow dropped in clumps from branches with leaves still holding on in the trees. She found it difficult moving through the drifts without snowshoes, but there were tracks from several small animals crisscrossing the terrain—rabbits searching for what saplings they might find, squirrels looking for the stash of acorns they had buried before the storm—and so she ventured farther down the mountain, too. At a stand of birch, she peeled off a knife's length of inner bark and thought of trying to make it to the hickory tree, but she was nearly spent from walking this short distance. She stopped beneath a white pine and gathered needles, then burrowed under the snow for cones. She found three and went back to the cave.

By evening, the food was gone. She sat before the fire and picked a scrawny nut from the last of the cones and threw the scales into the embers. They flared up for a moment, then disappeared. Outside, the wind blew across the mountain in a cry that reminded her of loons. She rose and placed the last of the dead cedar on the fire, knowing it would burn down long before morning came, and felt the gnaw of hunger.

When you talked to her on nights like these, the girl asked, huddled in her bed of blanket and skins between the rocks of the firepit and the wall of the entrance to the cave, what did she say back to you?

THE STORM WAS EARLY FOR THE SEASON, SHE KNEW. She had done rough measurements during her journey with the bear and could see the sun had not passed the winter solstice, for her shadow continued to lengthen along the ground. The animals had been caught off guard as well. That was why she had seen the tracks. But the cold had come early with the snow, and as she struggled to revive the fire in the morning her mind began turning over thoughts of sun and shade moving across the surface of the noon mark on the stone by the lake, branches bending in a breeze, rabbits cautious as they hopped out of the woods in the evening to eat from the tall grass along the shore, then no rabbits at all, and her father telling her that the rabbits and hares the hawks had not found would be harder to hunt now. Snow in late fall, fish, too, gone from the weir. We'll have to wait until the ice is thick before we can catch them, he had said, meaning rabbits, hares, and fish. She remembered the man teaching her how to build a snare that fall, and the warmth of the stove in the small house rising with the smell of roasting game.

She stood then, took a piece of charcoal from the fire, and began to make marks on the cave wall. How long from the last moon? The length of her shadow when she last looked up at noon?

Two things alone demanded her attention. Food and home. All of the materials she needed for a snare were in the pack she carried and out there in the woods. Sticks, cordage, and a knife. If the rabbits, too, were foraging before winter set in, she could lead those rabbits into a trap. And if the days remained this cold, the river she and her father had walked along for almost a full moon, going north to cross, could be crossed now over ice without having to trek into the high mountains. It would be a shorter trip home this far south, one she could make by the solstice.

She left the cold firepit and emptied all but the wrapped and bound bones and ash from her pack. She placed her hand inside and palm down on the folded deerskin she had never seen him without, and said, I will not stop until I bury you beside her. I promise.

ALL THAT DAY SHE SPENT PREPARING FOR THE next, then returned in the morning to the place where she had seen the rabbit tracks. She chose a spot along a path that showed fresh tracks and where there was a bendable tree. She trimmed it for length and used the trimmings for the frame of the snare on the ground and for the trigger, then attached the cordage to the trigger and the tree. She tied a slipknot in the cord, bent the tree down, and set the snare, using beech tree leaves and wintergreen berries for bait. Then she moved off in the direction of the hickory tree, where she was determined to find food.

She was out until early evening, so leaden was her progress in the snow, and returned with the front of her wrap folded up and holding hickory nuts, pinecones, and a handful of more wintergreen berries she had found nestled among moss.

She left these at the cave and returned in the last of the waning light to where she had set the snare, and found a live cottontail dangling from the sapling she had bent across the path. She watched it for a moment before approaching and thought she heard a cry, then took out her knife and walked up to the tree. She could see a spark of fear in the animal's eyes as it struggled to get free, and she lifted it so that it was no longer hanging.

I'm sorry, she whispered, and moved fast with the knife.

SHE ATE HALF OF THE MEAT SHE ROASTED THAT night and wrapped the rest in leaves. Then she scraped and cleaned the inside and outside skin so that she could cure it and make a pair of mittens if she snared another. The dark had long settled by the time she was finished. She had foraged and hunted in one day what she thought would have taken three. She went outside for wood she had brought back from her expedition but first climbed the rocks at the top of the cave, where she had an expansive view of the night sky. A quarter moon had long set in the west and to the north shone lights of green and yellow and red that shimmered and waved like water across the upper air of the horizon. She gazed in wonder at the lights, at what could be alive there that high in the sky, and she felt a strength of will in her. She turned and looked south as though to memorize the way down the mountain. If she had had time, she might have made some snowshoes. But there was no time, not if she wanted to return before all the mountain paths became impassable.

STARS STILL FILLED THE MORNING SKY WHEN she rose and took a sip of her water and walked to the back wall, where the bear slept. She put her hand on his head and said, I can't wait here all winter, or I'll die.

The bear rolled over and the girl stepped back, expecting him to open his eyes and wish her a fond farewell, or plead with her not to go. He opened the loop of his body, rolled until he came to rest on the other side, and closed the loop again, snoring away with the slow rising and falling of his great bulk. She could see the depth of his sleep now, a sleep beneath the heavy lids that twitched in what half-light made its way to the back of the cave, a sleep in which he traveled through some unknown forest, or perhaps found his rest among the constellations of the night sky.

WHEN SHE STEPPED OUTSIDE, THE SKY HAD lightened and the woods seemed to have burgeoned in the dawn, so that she felt for one disorienting moment as though it were early spring, this snow the last of the snows, until the wind cut through the skin she wore and she knew it was winter.

She followed the same path down the mountain that she and the bear had taken to get to the cave and found herself covering ground she remembered. She used the sun along the ecliptic and her compass as a wayfinder, journeying south, where she picked up the creek that passed through the grove and over the falls, and then she turned west.

And when the sun through high clouds looked as though it was approaching midday, she stopped in an open grove to eat and measure her shadow in intervals. When she did this the next day, she found no increase at all, or so she believed, and called that day the winter solstice. She carried with her the sticks she had fashioned and used for her snare, and on the largest one she carved a mark with her knife. The first day. This would be her calendar now.

AFTER THREE DAYS OF WALKING IN HEAVY SNOW, stopping only to sleep, forage for food, and fill her water gourd, she came to the edge of the wide and frozen river, its banks framed by plains of meadow and forests where leafless birch and willow grew, the riparian world looking like sheets of white that twisted through the bottom of a shallow valley. She approached to test the ice. Her father had taught her how to discern the thickness by color and water type. She brushed back the snow cover on the surface, the ice cloudy and grainy between, and lay down on her belly to spread her weight and listen. Each day since the storm, the air had been below freezing. On the lake, that would have been enough for a hand's length of ice. She had never seen a frozen river, though. She rose on all fours and crawled out a little farther, lay down on her belly again, listened, and crawled out another five steps on her knees. Then she stood and walked out three more. It was not a fast river when she had last seen it, but it was deep. Yet all around her now was ice. There were no open areas where rapids might have kept the surface from thickening, no ice jams where wind and rapids both would have pushed up a floe wall and left a broad pocket of air underneath. She moved toward the far shore, no farther away from where she stood than the house was from the lake, and felt that distance like a pull. She knelt down to look once more at the surface, then stood.

For some time that day she had felt that something was following her. When she had stopped to eat, or when she had come to a narrowing of the path. It wasn't anything she heard, only felt. And now she wanted to cross the river as much to be away from a land in which she had spent more time than she had ever believed possible as to return to where time passed in a place familiar, even if it were familiar now to her alone.

She took four more steps toward the shore, put her arms out as if to fly, and set out across the ice, first at a trot, then running as fast as she could over the snowpack that shrouded the river.

THERE WAS NO CRACK, NO MOVEMENT, NO SOUND like a moan. The ice exploded and she fell through as though she were a stone, a gasp of surprise the only air she took with her as she shot down.

The water was dark, the cold unbearable and tightening like a bowstring around her chest. She twisted to look for the light from the hole and saw it slanting through the broken ice. She stroked hard against the current as it pulled on her, pulled down, and yet she was not swept away by it. Something was holding her, and she remembered the pack. It had caught on the underside of the frozen river. She lifted her head above the water into the air pocket beneath the ice, breathed, and began to work her way back to the hole through which she had fallen. The cold was seeping into her now and she felt the pain of it in her head and body like a hammer blow. She inched her way beneath the ice, and when the hole looked within reach, she thrust her arms out, dived beneath the water to release the pack, and kicked hard, knowing there would be little air or strength left in her to swim back if she could not get her hands on the edge. She kicked again against the current and grabbed the jagged shelf, her frozen legs finning back and forth underwater as she held on and climbed out and onto the river ice.

She felt a bite at the back of her neck then, as if her shoulders had been placed in a soft vise, and her body lifted, her frozen limbs dragging across the snow, ice beneath her and what carried her cracking in unison as they kept moving faster and faster toward the shore, a warm breath at the place of the bite the only warmth she felt now, felt with a tenderness and an urgency as she drifted and came to rest on snow and frozen river grass.

So this is death, she thought, yet knew somehow that even this was not true and tried to stand, when a towering puma with fur like gold outlined in black and a nose in the shape of a rising dove the color of sumac tucked a paw beneath her and lifted her, pulled her into the soft warm down of its chest, and began to run across the plain and back into the forest.

*S*HE SWAM UP, SANK DOWN, AND SWAM UP *again, finding she was able to breathe this time in the water of the dream. When her head breached the surface, she looked across the lake and saw her father paddling away from her in the old birch-bark canoe. She began to swim with strong, even strokes, as she had done on summer afternoons as a girl, until her arms tired and she could not lift them from her sides, and she began sinking again, the water becoming colder and colder, the surface drifting away above her and dimming like a weakening fire.*

SHE WOKE BETWEEN TWO BODIES OF FUR, THE bristles of the sleeping bear and the soft pelt of the puma, the cat's arms cradling her still to keep her off of the cold cave floor.

She stretched out along the body of the bear, and the puma moved to let her sit up slowly on her own and look around. Full daylight poured in

from the cave mouth, and the girl tried to stand
once more and face that light, but she could not.
She felt her shoulders for the pack and found it
still there. She still wore the shoes her father
had made for her. She turned to the wall and
regarded the bear breathing in his slumber like
an enormous bellows, his body rising and falling
and bent in the open curve of a waxing crescent
moon. Then she turned to the puma framed in
daylight. Again she tried to stand, but her legs
buckled and she sat back down and hugged herself to keep from shivering, then looked up and
watched the puma slip out of the cave.

IT WAS A LONG TIME BEFORE SHE COULD STAND
and walk. She moved to the front of the cave and
found everything she needed to raise a new fire
in the pit—tinder, kindling, and logs, gathered
and dry on the stones. She drank what water
remained in her gourd, took off her pack, and
searched inside for her flint and steel, which she
worked to spark the tinder until she had a flame
and the kindling was burning. Then she took

from the pack her wet blanket and bedding and spread them out to dry.

By the afternoon, she was in front of that blaze still, having risen only to find more wood and to collect pine needles for tea, which she drank with her hands cupped around the pannikin she carried like an ember banked and holding what heat she longed to hold within herself. She glanced to the back of the cave at the bear, as though waiting for him to wake and tell her this was all part of another dream, one from which she would wake. But the bear slept on.

SHE WAS ASLEEP ON THE CAVE FLOOR, THE FIRE small dances of flames on the burnt tips of logs, when the puma returned, nudged the girl awake, and walked back outside. The girl stirred and stood and followed into the gray twilight.

On the ground in the snow lay a deer, eyes glassy and empty of flight, antlers broken off, and the fur at the neck darkened with frozen blood. The puma sat licking its paws while the girl studied the kill. Then she knelt down, closed the deer's eyelids, and unsheathed her knife.

She worked slowly and with what care she knew to give the animal as she dressed it. Twilight had waned to dusk by the time she was done, the waxing moon rising over the trees in the east. She would wait until morning to carve it and skin it, but she pulled the offal away from the carcass now, propped open the chest cavity with a stick, and pushed snow into the opening. Then, from the ground where she had scooped the snow, she dug up a rock with a flat side, cleaned the dirt from it, and knelt back down in front of the deer. She felt inside the chest for the center bone and, with the rock, began to strike the sternum until it broke. She wedged the rock into the break and levered it open until she could get both hands and her knife into the cavity. She held it now, still warm somehow, cut away the muscle and arteries that kept it in place, and pulled the deer's heart out, so big that she had to hold it in both hands.

He taught you well, said the puma, its voice raspy and slow.

The girl turned to stare at the big cat, not surprised that it would speak to her but that the

animal knew she had learned to do this from her
father.

What would you like while my knife is sharp?
the girl asked.

I've had my fill, the cat said.

INSIDE THE CAVE, THE GIRL BUILT UP THE FIRE
and made a small oven of stone at the edge of
the coals, in which she placed the deer's heart.
No other words passed between her and the
puma. She waited in the quiet for the meat to
cook, then ate her supper with a hunger she'd
never known, washed her hands and face in the
snow, then took her place by the fire again until
she fell asleep against the stone over which she
had draped her bedding.

IN THE MORNING, THE PUMA WAS GONE. THE GIRL
had saved a quarter of the heart and this she ate
with melted snow, then walked outside to look
at the deer carcass in daylight. It was all there.
Food. A hide. Sinew for a bowstring and thread.
Bones for sewing needles, arrowheads, and a

smaller fishhook if she could carve it. She would look for a medium oak in the forest, cut it down, and make a new bow. It wouldn't be as good as the one her father had made, but it would be good enough. She cleared the snow she had packed in the chest cavity and set about skinning the deer, paring out the meat, and cutting the sinew from the backstrap and four legs. Half of the meat she packed with snow and stored in a large crack in the cave wall. The rest she put aside to smoke. The sinew she cleaned and put near the fire to dry. Then she turned to the hide.

On a large, smooth, and sloping stone she fleshed the hide with her knife and cleaned it. When she was finished, she went in search of branches and sticks for a drying rack and built a crude one out of deadfall pressed into crevices and propped up against the roof of the cave, and with the cordage from her pouch she stretched and tied the skin to the rack, where she would let it set until the moon was full.

When she came out of the cave, the puma stood by the entrance with two dead possum. The girl took them by their tails and began to dress them, one after the other, carving up what meat she could find on them before she fleshed these fur hides, too, with her knife, set them near the fire to dry, and opened the skulls of the possums for the brains she would use to cure the skins.

She finished at midday and cooked a cut of venison for her meal. The puma had disappeared again, so the girl banked the fire and went out to look for a tree that would make a good bow.

She returned close to twilight, carrying only a dried branch she had found for the fire. The puma once more stood by the cave. Two large beavers were facedown in front of her. The girl picked them up to inspect them, and the puma rasped, They'll wait. Sit down. There are some things I want to tell you before I have to go.

The girl broke the branch over her knee, walked into the cave, and placed the largest piece of it on the fire.

The puma did not go inside this time, but paced at the entrance of the cave, stopping to look up at the mountain every now and then as though wary or waiting, then stood still in the half-light and told the girl there was more winter to come and that although she knew the way home from here, it was not the time to make her way home, if she wished to return to the mountain that stands alone to bury her father. The cat had given her enough food for some weeks, and fur she could use to keep warm while hunting if she used what skills she had to cure the hides. The rest was all around, in the forest that did not die in winter but only changed.

Look at the bear, the puma said to the girl. On and on he sleeps, but in his dreams he wanders as he did awake, going back over the paths of forests he once knew, paths he walked with you, telling you much about the things others like you never knew or cared to know. You are bound to him now, as closely as you are to the bones you carry. If you don't wake, this cave will be your tomb, and the bear will carry with him when he wanders a memory of an autumn when he traveled for a time with one who carried grief. But if you do wake and journey home, the bear and a line of bears after him will carry the story of the last one's return to the mountain that stands alone. Carry it for the forest to remember for as long as there is forest beneath the sun.

The girl did not look up when the puma finished speaking. Her eyes remained fixed on the fire. The sky had become overcast and the smoke of the fire no longer drew straight, but wandered in waves between the pit and the ground, a harbinger of more snow to come. She reached up and eased the straps of the pack from her shoulders, stood, and walked with it to the back wall, where she left it on the floor next to the sleeping bear.

When she turned toward the cave entrance and the fire again, she watched the puma slip from that light into the dark.

WIND AND BLINDING SNOW KEPT HER inside and huddled around her firepit all of the next morning. She had a breakfast of weak sassafras tea and venison and marked the cave wall now for a calendar, starting with when she first began counting from the solstice at the river, then adding five more for the three she was asleep and the two she was awake with the puma. She paced the stone floor, listening to the slow and rumbling breathing of the bear, and thought of what the puma had said about being bound to him. She felt bound to nothing but her desire to be home and would cling to this and this alone to survive. She dressed and fleshed the skins of the beavers and set them to dry, then took the possum furs and washed the skin side in a bath of the animals' brains, wrung them and stretched them and built up the fire with green wood to smoke them so they'd be soft as they dried one last time.

SHE COULD GO NOWHERE IN THE FOREST WITHOUT good snowshoes, and the pine limbs and hemlock boughs she needed to make them were not far from the cave. There was a break in the storm as noon approached and so she trudged outside into snow up to her knees and made her way down to the tree line. She climbed the first white pine she saw and broke four branches from the trunk and placed them standing up in the snow. Then she slogged farther down the mountain to a stand of hemlock and cut from it as many boughs as she could carry, dragged branches and boughs through drifts back to the cave, and set to work.

She used the jagged edge of a rock splintered in the fire to cut the branches to chest height, and used her knife to carve a flat end on one side and a notch on the other. With the leg sinew from the deer she lashed four smaller sticks crosswise to the center of the branches for foot supports, then bent the ends of the branches together until they touched at the flat and lashed these, too. When she was done, she had two fish-shaped snowshoes half her size. She took the hemlock boughs and wove them in from the back of the shoe, under the foot supports and out at the front, so that they fit snug and tight within the pine frames. She placed them on the floor and stood on them and knew they would hold her.

FIVE DAYS THE STORM LASTED, DURING WHICH she lived on venison and tree bark. She took half of the meat she kept in snowpack and smoked it on the rack she had made for the skins, whittling green maple saplings into chips and cold-smoking the venison as she had watched her father do. This took a day and a night, and she wondered if the smoke she made for skins and meat would wake the bear, but the animal slept on.

The morning of the sixth day she woke to sun and bitter cold. She built up the fire with the last of her logs, chewed on a piece of deer for breakfast, then tied her snowshoes to her feet and walked outside.

The forest was a world of silence. Deep snow had buried all that was in it but the trees, and it looked to her like the world outside her father's house in seasons when the snow fell there, too, for days at a time and they waited for storms to stop, then built up their own fire, put on snow-shoes made of wood and skins, and stepped out-side. No wind blew. No living thing of any kind moved, except the girl. She stamped her shoes to test their lashings and her weight, and listened to the sound of the *thump* echoing down the moun-tain in the cold. Then she walked slowly across the new ground.

SHE THOUGHT OF THE PUMA AND HOW IT HAD kept turning to look up at the mountain as it paced back and forth and spoke to her. She had never climbed up, only down, toward what opportunity to forage the forest had to offer. There was something up there, and she wanted to see what it was.

The climb was steeper than she expected, but her snowshoes held together and kept her mov-ing quickly over the deep drift-covered ground. She needed warmer clothing. The blanket and old deerskin she wore were not enough. She knew now why the puma had brought her the possum and beaver. She would sew the fur skins into a hat and mittens when she got back to the cave in the evening. If she could capture enough of them, she would sew rabbit and hare onto the inside of the deerskin shirt she wore, too. Anything to keep her warmer longer. There were many winter days ahead of her that would be colder than even this one.

She hadn't climbed far when the path up the mountain became so steep she had to take off her snowshoes. She thought of turning back but knew she would not get many chances to make this summit when it wasn't snowing or bitter cold. Seeing the lay of the land around her would help her identify landmarks that she would need when she went out to hunt. She left her snowshoes by an exposed ledge and hiked on, bouldering with hands and feet, the way becoming more and more difficult, until she came to a sheer rock face that was blown clear of snow and broken in two down the middle, so that a kind of wide open chimney reached through the rock to the top. She stepped inside the gap, leaned her back against one side of the chimney and placed her feet against the other. Then she began to inch her way up, her hands and back flat against the cold face of the rock, her body slowly sliding up the crevice at an angle. When she came to the top, she lunged forward, grabbed the lip of the rock, and pulled herself up onto the snow-covered summit.

She looked out on a scene so similar to what she had seen from the mountain she called home, it was as if she were standing at the same place she had stood on the first day her father had taken her to her mother's grave, but for the snow. And yet this could not be the mountain that stands alone. There was no bear-shaped cap. No lake in the distance. No roof of a house and twist of smoke rising from it. No cairn of memorial stones.

It was the landscape below that was different. As she looked south, she could see the unmistakable frozen and snow-covered path of the river winding for miles through the forest. She could see where the path she had taken with the bear intersected it, and she could see the floodplains next to the woods and the wide section of the river that opened up there, all signs of her attempt at crossing erased and frozen over. This was where she would winter. This was where she would live or die, roaming the forest in search of food, sleeping in a cave.

I need a bow, she said out loud, slid back into the narrow stone chimney, and climbed down.

When she returned to the cave, she built up the fire and made another oven of stone, into which she placed the last cut of raw venison and surrounded it with coals. She melted snow in a cup and let it heat, then brewed in it a handful of pine needles for tea.

She ate half of the meat, wrapped the rest in leaves, and put it in the pouch she carried. Then she turned to the back of the cave and said, I'm going down the mountain to look for a tree I can carve into a bow.

She picked up her water gourd, knife, and the fire-split stone she used as a saw.

I'll be as long as it takes, she said, and left the cave.

The whisper of her snowshoes drifting down the mountain was all the sound there was in the forest, and she moved at an almost rhythmic trot to the tree line and into the cover of the hemlock and pine, then on down farther into the groves of birch and taller hardwoods. She had been over this ground so much, she knew what she sought was not among the trees there. It would be her height, and so it would be close to the mature trees, but at enough of a distance from their shadows to grow.

She began to angle back up the mountain and walk in circles that opened out, taking her over new ground outside of the path she and the bear had followed from the river. And when she had made the fourth and largest pass, she saw a birch that had bent down and snapped under the heavy snow. She stopped and sat on it as she would on a bench and listened to the creaks and groans of the old trees farther away in the forest as they listed almost imperceptibly in the cold, their sapless bark and long limbs seeming to stretch and ache, too, in their slow, slow wait for spring.

She remembered the bear had said it would take a full phase of the moon to listen to the trees, and she wondered if this was an exaggeration or if this was so. She would freeze or starve or both if he was right. Her hands and head covered with fur now, her feet dry and warm on their hemlock boughs, she thought, I'll be as long as it takes, and stared out at the stark landscape of the forest. She wondered—as she had wondered when she was a girl of what a bear might say if it were to speak to her—what trees in winter might tell her, if she could learn to listen, or learn to see.

It would have happened all the same had she not been there, for wind direction changed all the time in the winter mountains, but where the wind had once been blowing a dried and brittle beech leaf across her path, it shifted around behind and the leaf turned and tumbled away. She stood from the log and let herself be pushed in the direction of that wind farther into the forest, away from the route of her circular path.

HER FATHER HAD TAUGHT HER TO MEASURE distance in strides of ten, and she reckoned she had walked a hundred of them before she stood next to the oak. It was thin and only slightly taller than she, yet it grew with a straightness and look of strength. She walked around it and inspected the bark, then surveyed the surrounding grove.

She was wrong about trees growing in their own light. There were several larger oaks nearby. This one seemed to grow not in their shade but under their protection. She walked back to the tree and held it as she would a bow. Her fingers just circled around it. There would be enough wood to work but not so much that it would take the rest of the winter to draw it down. And she would have to do this with the sapwood still green, working it and leaving it by the fire each day before it was a bow she could use.

She loosened her fingers then and held the tree gently, in the way her father used to hold her hand. She thought of the bear and what he had told her about the forest by the riverside. And she remembered the day her father had presented her with staves of hickory in his woodshed, having found them and timbered them in the forest when she was five. I was waiting for you to be ready, he had said.

She knelt down and cleared snow away from the base of the tree, took her mitten off, and touched the thin trunk with her bare hand.

I just hope it's not the last winter for both of us, she said.

Then she felled the tree as close to the ground as she could chop with her rock, trimmed its branches, and walked with it back to the bent-down birch. From this she took what good arrow limbs she could find and hiked up the mountain.

IN THE CAVE, SHE REMOVED THE BARK FROM THE oak and put the stave at a distance from the fire. Then she took up the dried backstrap sinew she had removed from the deer the puma had killed and with her comb began to separate and tease out the fibers, which she wove into string, twisting and pinching them together, working in more sinew each time she came to the end of a strand, until the cordage was the length of the stave and she tied the bitter end into a loop.

She was finished by evening. She chewed on a piece of smoked possum for her supper and made another cup of tea, then built up the fire and walked in the moonlight down the mountain to the tree line and set her snare with wintergreen leaves in another stand of hemlock, where she hoped rabbits would come to forage at dawn.

In the morning, she found a white varying

hare dangling from the trip wire. She killed it, dressed it, and skinned it in the snow. Back in the cave, she prepared the hide and fur for drying and placed the meat on a spit to slow-cook over coals. Then she gave the rest of the day to her bow.

THE WOOD WAS GREEN AND STRONG AND IT TOOK a great deal of drawing down and carving with her knife to get a flat, even curve to the inside of the bow. She could have tapered the ends, put nocks in them, and made quick, straight arrows to shoot, but she took her time. One day turned into three as she sighted and carved, sighted and carved, giving the bow some extra set by holding it in place with rocks overnight by the fire.

When she was finished, she strung the bow with sinew and tillered it from the crotch of a tree. It was balanced better than she had expected and the draw weight felt strong enough to give a good arrow some speed and accuracy. She went back to the cave and smoothed the sides and handle with a round stone, then leaned the bow against the wall.

She carved and trimmed two arrows from the birch limbs, cut nocks into the string ends, and tied deer-bone arrowheads to the tips. What she lacked were feathers. Her father had told her once that pine needles would serve as adequate fletching for an arrow, if no feathers could be found, so she went outside and took some needles from a white pine, broke off a branch for the sap, and wrapped the needles around the upper shaft of each arrow with thin strands of sinew and warmed sap for glue. When she was finished, she held one arrow in each hand, balancing them lightly in the center with her fingers. Then she sighted down the shafts. She would just have to get close to whatever game she was after.

SHE ROSE BEFORE FIRST LIGHT AND SNOWSHOED down the mountain and back to the place where she had cut the young oak for the bow and sat in a birch stand, one arrow nocked, another on the ground at the ready.

At dawn, a small, blithe doe walked into the grove through the snow, nibbling at the low-lying branches of a maple, which held little if anything of sustenance for the animal. The girl was tired and hungry herself, but she held her bow steady as she drew back, aimed for the heart above the shoulder, and let go.

The doe looked up at the sound of wind whistling past, then turned back to the twigs of maple. The girl nocked the other arrow, drew back, and missed again. She stood from her blind and the doe turned, sniffed the air, and bounded away into the denser growth.

DAYS GREW COLDER ON THE MOUNTAIN AND NOT a night passed without snowfall, so that it looked to the girl when she ventured out now as though the forest itself was losing inhabitants, the smaller trees and rock piles that had been landmarks to her only days before disappearing beneath the cover of the deep snow.

She collected what birch limbs she could find and shaped these into arrows, until she had a quiver of six, including the two she had shot at the doe and retrieved. Each morning she left the cave in search of food to kill. Each evening she returned with nothing but hunger, her strength sapped by the hard snowshoe trek up and down the mountain, her body kept from winnowing entirely by the leaves and tree bark she ate, the pine-needle tea she brewed and drank. She could not get close enough to deer or squirrel or even hare to take a shot that would not go wide or bury itself in the snow, and the bait she would have used if she had set a snare, she ate for food herself. She saw less and less game each day, so wary and scarce had the animals become as the winter wore on, and then she saw no game at all.

S HE WOKE TO HUNGER. THE FIRE WAS ASH AND coals. She stood slowly and picked up her bow and quiver and put on her snowshoes. At the mouth of the cave, she ate the new snow that had fallen in the night and walked down the mountain, alert only to the cold, and wandered from groves where she had set snares that were empty now to rocks behind which she had hidden and lain in wait for deer that no longer came.

From the morning past midday, she walked the mountain, the slope of it and the wind, more than her legs and feet, carrying her down. She spoke to her father as she meandered, slow and hunched, assuring him she had not gone so far that she could not return and that the promise she had made would endure, as she would, no matter how cold or hungry. She told him to wait with the bear. She had to rest if she was going to have the strength to find food and get back to him.

Just some water, she thought, and sat and

lapped up handfuls of snow, which melted in her mouth. She was so far down the mountain now that the sun had gone behind the summit, though it was light out still. And sleep, more sleep she said to herself. She eased her body into the deep-packed snow behind a stone around which grew some tall hickory, and she closed her eyes and listened to the stillness.

A SMALL DRIFT OF SNOW FROM A HICKORY LIMB dropped on the wind and fell on her face, and she sat up and looked over the top of the stone. It was near dusk. Her clothes were wet and her body was aching with cold. She gazed up the mountain slope to see how far she had walked, when she saw the scrawny hare upwind of her chewing on the twigs of a branch that had broken off and fallen onto the surface of the snow. The hare came in and out of focus as the girl squinted in the dim light but did not move. Then in one motion she slid an arrow from her quiver, nocked it, drew, and let go. The arrow rose on its pine-needle fletching, glanced off the branch, and hit the hare in the neck, knocking it over, so that it lay dazed in a growing pool of blood. The girl stumbled to her feet and raced toward it, snatched it up off the snow, and sucked at its neck wound through fur and fleas, the hare kicking wildly in its last throes against the girl's wrists as she tightened her grip, twisting the animal to wring it of life so that its neck snapped, and still she drank of that life until it was gone, then loped as fast as she could in her snowshoes with the bow on her shoulder and dragging the hare by its ears back up the mountain to the cave.

HER HANDS SHOOK AS SHE LAID A THIN OUTER layer of birch bark over the last embers she could find in the pit and blew until the bark smoked and caught fire. She put more bark, twigs of pine, and dried cedar she had scrounged onto the flames, and they rose. Then she took her knife and gutted and skinned the hare where she sat, the blood of the animal mixing with her own from the wrist scratches and a cut on her palm she suffered in her haste with the knife. She threw the skin off to the side and ran a stick through the carcass and placed it over the fire, turning it, watching the meat blacken and smoke, the smell of the burnt flesh filling the cave, and she could watch no longer. She pulled the meat out of the fire and tore off bites from the bones and swallowed them whole, then held her stomach and began to wretch and vomit over and over, until she could not breathe, and she vomited still, gasping and choking on blood and uncooked meat. Then she dropped to the floor on her hands and knees and huddled in the pool of her own mess on the stone, gasping and heaving until her breathing settled and she began to weep in her exhaustion and loneliness and fear now of all—even sleep.

SHE GAZED FROM THE TOP OF THE MOUNTAIN THAT stands alone. It was a day in late spring, the trees below a verdant green, above her an eagle flying in wide circles. In the distance she could see the small house and then she was standing inside the house, but her father was not there. She began to move around and found the hearth cold, spiderwebs in the corners, and mouse droppings on the floor. Then it was winter, snow blowing and drifting against the windows, the house empty still. She opened the door to leave and walked from the house into the cave. A bear was sitting next to the fire. He had a fish in his claws and he held it out to her.

Cook this, he said, and she placed it on the fire and in that moment it was done, but the girl could not move her arms to take the fish and eat.

You're hungry, I know, said the dreambear, but you need to be hungry for more than food. More than sleep. We all go to sleep and will be asleep for a long time. Be hungry for what you have yet to do while you're awake.

I can't live if I can't eat, said the girl.

You approached the river too early.

She looked down at the fish.

I can cross it now.

Crossing alone won't save you.

But I am alone.

The girl turned to the back of the cave and saw the bear still asleep in his curve against the wall.

You're not him, are you? she said to the dreambear.

You know who I am.

SHE WOKE AND CRAWLED OUTSIDE INTO morning, washed with snow, and ate handfuls of it to quench her thirst, then brought armfuls of it into the cave and threw it on the floor, where she had lain in her own vomit. Then she picked the half-eaten hare on the spit out of the ashes of the pit and raised a fire again, the warmth of it enough to melt the snow on the floor, so that it soaked with the smell of bile into cracks of stone.

She walked to the back of the cave then and from her pack took the pot her father had carried and threw in it what salt was left, shucked the hare's meat from the spit into the pot, and went outside to fill it with snow, then left it at the mouth of the cave. She put on her snowshoes and walked down to the tree line, where she shaved two handfuls of the cambium bark from a white pine. With this and a dried branch she broke off from the pine, she went back to the cave, placed the bark in the pot with the hare's meat, and stoked the flames with pieces of the branch.

She rested and drank water while her meager stew cooked. When the bark was soft and the meat had separated from the bones of the hare, she took the pot off the fire, cooled it in snow, and ate what she could of her dinner until she was sated but still weak. She knew now her only chance was to go back to the river and fish through the ice. If she could get there living on melted snow, moss, and tree bark, more chances for food would be along the river. And if she was lucky, there would be fish.

It was somewhere near midday. Hunger would find her again walking or in the cave, so she took her bow and quiver, cinched up her pack, and set out down the mountain once again on her snowshoes.

THE FIRST NIGHT, SHE MADE A FIRE WITH THE coals she carried and heated what was left of her bark and hare stew. The next morning, she wrapped up new coals from the fire and journeyed on.

She arrived at the riverside before evening of the third day and saw the place where she had tried to cross, the bank to which the puma had dragged her, the grasses in which she had once lain now covered in snow, out of which poked long stalks of goldenrod dotted with gall balls, and she remembered what her father had told her they held in winter. She walked out on the plain and began to pick the balls from the stems, then sat down and opened them with her knife. Inside each was a tiny white larva. She ate six of them with handfuls of snow. Then she took a small hook she had carved from a bone of the deer the puma had brought her and placed three of the larvae on the hook and tied it to the fishing line.

She knew that beneath the snow and ice there would be stones, and these the girl uncovered and sorted through for long sections of granite that she could hold like a chisel. She found two good ones of differing lengths and a round stone that fit in the palm of her hand for a mallet.

SHE COULD WALK ACROSS THE RIVER NOW, BUT SHE went out seven strides and set her fishing line and bait in the snow, cleared a section down to the ice, then etched a circle and began to chop with the stones. The ice was several hands thick and she chopped for a long time before water began to flow up through the hole her chisel had made, and she put it down so as not to lose it on the next strike. She took the other, longer length of stone and with this finished breaking through, clearing the hole of ice shards until she could see the river water below.

She picked up the line and dropped the hook through the hole, jigging the larvae bait up and down in the water through the ice. Right away she felt a tug and pulled up a small river chub. She still had bait on the hook and did this again, until she had three more chubs and the larvae were gone. Then she ran the hook through the lower and upper lip of one of the chubs and dropped this for bait into the water, letting the line out downriver so that the minnow would appear to be swimming upstream. She played the line as it drifted into deeper currents beneath the ice, and when the trout hit, she knew it was a big fish.

All three chubs caught fish for her. That evening, she built a fire with the winter brush and dead uprooted trees abundant on the river plain and cooked two of the trout. She ate everything but the bones of the fish and tended the fire into the night, until she fell asleep in her skins and blanket under the stars.

IN THE MORNING, SHE HARVESTED MORE GALL FLY larvae and landed four trout before the sun had risen above the trees in the east. From where she stood on the frozen river she could see weather coming from the north and she tried to decide if she should go back to the cave for its cover, or shelter in the woods near the river, where the food was, and she knew she would stay.

She walked back to the fire with her catch, gutted one, and placed it over green twigs to cook, at which point she looked up and saw an eagle perched on a low dead branch of an oak tree at the edge of forest and plain. It was a beautiful bird. Head and tail feathers a soft ivory against the wings' gray-black, its hooked beak and narrow talons the yellow of the sun rising above a bank of clouds. The whole of the bird looked as though it, too, had risen up out of the horizon of barren landscape entire and remained motionless in a perpetual attitude of study and hunt. The girl left her trout on the fire and walked toward the bird. The eagle shifted and ruffled its wings and she could see that it carried something in its claws. Then its head peered out and wings flapped and it soared from the branch down to the girl, dropped a goose it held in its talons onto the snow, and flew off in a tight circle back to the tree.

The girl picked up the goose. It wasn't a fresh kill, nor was it old. The long neck was broken at an angle and the head hung limp, blood frozen around its mouth. She looked up at the eagle and waved with her arm for it to come in. The bird alighted again on the oak branch and soared straight for the girl. She picked the largest of the trout she had caught and threw it as high above her as she could, and before the fish had even begun to descend, the eagle swooped and caught it in its talons and flew off in a straight line over the river to the far shore, disappearing into the forest to the west.

By evening, the front had passed, leaving only a dusting of snow. The girl made a lean-to out of pine and hemlock boughs on the path halfway to the bear, and she plucked the goose of its feathers and roasted it over a fire she started with dried goldenrod and kept burning all night with the deadfall of beech and oak she collected along the way.

When she returned to the cave the next day, she gutted her trout and placed them on the smoke rack and raised a fire once again in the cold pit on the stone floor. And when the room had warmed, she took the six arrows from her quiver, stripped them of the pine-needle fletching, and scraped all of the sap from the upper shaft. With her knife she cut grooves in the shafts for the goose feathers, split the feathers, and attached them to the arrows. She inspected the deer-bone heads, and replaced two of them with the glass arrowheads she had made on the beach with the pieces her father had dug from the dirt at the place of the walls. Then she laid all of her arrows out along the floor near the fire to dry.

It was late afternoon and she had used up what strength she had. But she felt nothing of the hunger she had felt for so long. There was goose and smoked trout to eat for more than a phase of the moon, and she felt an altogether different hunger for the hunt rise along with her strength. She knew the arrows she made and held in her quiver now would fly, if she could track what game was out there and come within range of shooting. She looked across the fire and saw her father sitting on the floor and staring into the flames and smoke. She closed her eyes and opened them again, and he was gone.

A PINK DAWN FLUSHED ACROSS THE MORNING snow as the girl emerged from the cave in her fur and skins with her bow and arrows, and it dissipated imperceptibly before the sun had broken the horizon line. Her father told her once that all animals were creatures of habit and so, too, were they. The difference was she could choose to change her habits. Animals changed when they were afraid. Change before fear has had a chance to overcome you, he said, or after you have overcome it and like a storm it has moved on. And so she climbed neither up nor down the mountain that morning, but followed the ridge, circling it as though to tie a cord around the mountain's middle.

AS THE SKY BRIGHTENED AND THE SUN ROSE higher, the girl was in forest she had never seen before, the trees thicker and rock formations

sheer and nearly bereft of vegetation, a dusting
of new fallen snow soft and powdery over the old
pack. She moved quickly in the snowshoes she
had become so accustomed to, following a natural path that began to rise onto a rocky ledge that
after a short distance opened up into a vista from
which she could see over the tops of the trees
that grew in the forest below.

The sun had risen clear in the sky and from
where she stood on the ledge she crouched down
to scan the slope, then put her hand to the ground
and felt the lip of rock. Frozen. She struck the
ice with the handle of her knife, and it broke
away easily, revealing water and moss underneath. She lay on her belly and could see a wall
of ice stretching from the ledge to the ground,
a stream she knew began in the vernal pools at
the mountaintop, seeped into the ground, and
traveled downslope, creating the ice sheet in
winter. She chipped at the ice and peeled away
what moss she could from the wall with the blade
of her knife, placed the moss in her pouch, then
stood and climbed down off the ridge as though
she were lifted over the snow.

SHE SAW IT WHEN SHE STOOD. A DENSE gathering of hardwoods far in the distance, growing in the rich ground that had slowly washed down the mountainside longer than any but the trees could remember. In that gathering there would be shelter for animals from the wind, and food—acorns, beechnuts, hickory, and samaras—shelter that would draw them to its floor, even this deep in winter.

She approached the grove in a wide arc so as not to spook any animal that might already be foraging, but the woods were quiet. She sat down near a grouping of beech and placed her bow on the ground. There she remained without moving for the entire day, with moss to eat and snow to drink. The sun disappeared behind the summit of the mountain and still she remained in the grove. Night found her in the same place.

SHE WOKE IN THE DARK AND LOOKED UP THROUGH the leafless branches. Leo was following the Bear in the high eastern sky. It was close to morning. She reached into her pouch, took some moss and ate it with snow, then stood slowly and placed her forehead against the smooth silver bark of the beech.

The light turned from gray to the silver of the trees and she felt as though she could feel the earth itself spinning. There was nothing in her now. No hunger, no sleep, no longing, and no cold. She understood what she had been told. She picked up her bow, nocked an arrow, and listened for the stag she knew was coming up the mountain to meet her.

WINTER DAY FOLLOWED UPON WINTER day, the snow and cold like a never-ending stream bent on engulfing the forest in one all-consuming freeze. But the girl was not daunted. She had tanned and sewn together a new pair of deerskin and rabbit-fur shoes, on the outside of which she placed the beaver tails for a sole. The rest of the furs, which she had cured, she sewed into the deerskin shirt she had worn when she first entered the forest, so that now she herself looked like some ragged and otherworldly animal trudging through the landscape, a quiver of arrows on her back and over her shoulder an oaken bow.

She hunted when her food supply was exhausted. Each time, she moved through the woods to a place where she had not hunted before. There she sat and listened to the forest, then waited and watched to see which animal gave itself. Her arrows were sharp, her bow powerful, and she aimed well. In her gratitude, she left behind tender branches, piles of moss, and wintergreen berries. If it was a big deer, she left a fair portion of the meat by the chimney crack on the mountaintop for the other carnivores, and always in the morning the food was gone.

When the storms came and she huddled in the cave around her fire, she knew, too, that all else huddled somewhere for warmth. Those were the hours during which she marked and counted with charcoal on the cave wall the phases of the moon, or noted the constellations visible in the sky, counting down to the equinox, when light and dark would be the same over the land. And each night before sleep by the firelight, she would speak to her father, telling him what she had done that day, what she planned to do the next, and that she hoped to be home on the solstice, as she had always been.

IN TIME, SHE FELT WINTER LOOSENING ITS GRIP, as it would have to. The days grew longer. The sun arced higher in the sky. The nights gave up their cold. One morning when the girl climbed to the summit of the mountain, she noticed the ice in the river had broken up. Even from so far away, she could make out mounds of it bunched and piled against both shores, water flowing down the middle of it like a course of metallic slurry.

We'll still have to cross in the high mountains, she said out loud, and climbed back down to the cave.

SHE WAITED UNTIL EARLY MORNING OF THE next day and set off down the same forest path toward the river. But she was faster and stronger. The journey that had taken three days two months ago took one full day. She was used to the path, and though the snow remained deep, with each stride she could feel her heart beat faster, as it had when she was younger and knew that winter was giving way to spring. She arrived by dusk at the riverbank.

She had her bow and the longest, thinnest cord from sinew she could twist to add some length to the fishing line she had tied to an arrow. But as she approached the water, she watched slabs of ice rise up and slide beneath other slabs in a constant jockeying across the entire river. Even if she could get close enough to stand on a rock and fire into a pool, the arrow would hit ice and break before it hit what fish might be swimming in the current below. So she ate the smoked venison she had brought with her and slept at the edge of the forest in a makeshift lean-to. The next day, she walked back to the cave.

When she gazed at the stars at night outside the cave, Cancer was the constellation directly above, with Gemini setting in the west and Leo rising. Mornings, she had begun to hear birdsong, and where the snow had disappeared on rock ledges, small shoots of grass emerged among the twisted cedar trees and tiny wildflowers bloomed. Night and day were balanced. Spring had come to the forest.

She let a phase of the moon pass and went back to the summit to see the river. The water was a uniform blue, its edges shades of white and green, with swaths of high grass reaching across the plain and into the woods. That night, she went to sleep, with everything she would need for an outing of a few days packed and ready.

The next day was warm and she moved without snowshoes, taking the path at a good run most of the way. The sun was still high and the light slanted but strong when she arrived at the river—the fourth time she had stood on its banks. She scanned the surface of the swift water, looking for a pool or a rock, the downstream pocket in which fish could rest and wait for food to pass by. She waded into the water and could feel the power of it pulling her. She took another step into water up to her knees, the current so strong that she had to lean upstream in order not to be knocked down. It was as cold as she remembered the icy water of the winter was, and if she went any farther, she'd be washed away again.

As she looked upstream, she could see where the surface smoothed and slowed around something submerged. She struggled in this direction against the current and saw that there was a large round rock beneath the surface. She shielded her eyes with her hands against the setting sun and could see through the roiling water the slow wavering tails of trout suspended in the slipstream. She nocked the deer-bone fishing arrow to which she had tied her line, aimed below where she had glimpsed those tails, and fired.

She felt the fish surge against the line, then fall back underwater right into her. She pulled it out and walked quickly over to the shore. It was a beautiful trout, almost as big as the striped fish that she had caught in the ocean. She eased the arrowhead out and left the fish flapping on the grass of the shore, then waded out to the same spot, nocked an arrow again, and waited.

She wasn't sure the other trout hadn't been spooked. The first one came downstream fast enough after she had hit it, and if the feeding lane was as good as she thought it was, other fish would be in there. Daylight was waning. Just as the sun hit the tip of the mountain range to the west, she aimed in the same spot and released the arrow into the water, where it stopped as though it had been shot into a block of wood.

The fish surged upstream, slackened, then tumbled back down into her. This trout was bigger than the first. The girl's knees and legs ached from the cold as she stumbled out of the water and onto the bank, soaking wet. But she gathered up her catch and walked to the edge of the forest, where the lean-to remained, and she still had coals enough to raise a fire.

IN THE MORNING, SHE PACKED THE SECOND FISH in snow and went down to the river for another try before she walked back to the cave. She did everything as before and caught nothing. The fish had moved. She ventured out into the water one more stride and could see that there was a similar rock next to the other one on the river bottom. The current through the gap between the two would be too fast, but not the pocket behind the other stone. It was a longer shot, but she had to take it. She had to know. She drew back and let go.

This time the fish bolted toward the middle of the river and took all of the line she had on the bow. She waded out to her chest and could feel the fish trying to wrest free of the arrow, the water pushing hard against her as she struggled to keep her balance. The fish gave up just as she slipped and was whisked down the river. She pushed the end of her bow into the water to lever herself toward shore and swam as hard as she could to the bank, until she could feel rocks and grass beneath her, then dragged herself and the fish onto the shore.

THE GIRL LEFT THE RIVER WITH FIVE FISH. She reached the cave by evening of the same day, cooked one for her supper, and went to sleep. In the morning, she brewed a cup of strawberry-leaf tea, and said to the bear, without turning to look at the back of the cave, Good fishing down there. But you knew that already.

She heard something then like a yawn and a growl come from the corner of the cave, and she turned, to see the bear sitting up and shaking his head, as though he had no idea where he was. Then he staggered to his feet and began to move in the direction of the light.

The girl rose and stepped out of his way as he walked from the cave and stopped at the rock wall, down which melting snow was trickling in a stream. He stood there lapping up the water, then walked onto the forest floor and began to devour the shoots of plants that had pushed up through the melting snow. After he had grazed on what he could find without venturing too far, he ambled back into the cave and lay down again.

He did this three more times over the next two days, staying outside longer to eat and drink each time. On the morning of the third day, he recognized the girl and sat down next to her by the fire.

Eat this, she said, and handed him a fish.

The girl watched as the bear consumed the fish down to the bones, turned to her, and asked, Do you have another?

She went outside to where she had packed in snow the fish she had caught and brought back from the river, uncovered one, and gave it to the bear. He ate it with the same ravenous attention as the other, threw the skeleton on the floor, and licked his claws when he was done, and the two sat quietly around the fire.

Long winter? the bear asked finally.

Cold and dark. You know, said the girl. Winter.

I don't know, said the bear. But the colder the

winter, the harder it is for me to climb out of my rest. I had a dream, though, and you were in it.

Tell me, said the girl.

We were sitting around a fire, like this one, talking about sleep. I was worried that when I woke I would find you in a long sleep and would have to bury you.

Here I am, said the girl.

Here I am, too, said the bear. And if you're keeping fish on ice out there, I would be much better company if I had one more.

The girl stood.

I have more than one, she said. But the river is full of them. When you're strong enough, I'll take you there.

FOUR DAYS LATER, THEY CLIMBED DOWN THE mountainside along the same path bear and girl had last trekked together in the autumn, the girl telling the bear about her adventures while he slept. She told him about the puma, and how the big cat had rescued her when she tried to cross on the thin ice and nearly drowned. She told him about the game the cat had brought her to eat. And she told him how she had made snowshoes and a bow, but even so could find no game to hunt or hit with the arrows she had made, and she was certain she would starve. Then she dreamed of a bear who had given her a fish, and she woke and went to the river to fish through the ice. That was when an eagle brought her a goose, whose feathers she used to make better arrows, and she began hunting again by speaking first to the forest and the animals, telling them of her gratitude for what they would give her, but knowing she could not have survived the winter without what she had been given, regardless of what she had made.

THEY TRAVELED AS FAR AS THE FOREST THAT bordered the river plain—the bear having to ask the girl to slow down so that he could catch up with her, for she was not walking so much as bounding and he still had some of the winter sleep in him—and stopped in a pine grove for the evening. There were shoots and leaf buds growing all around now for both the girl and the bear to eat. The bear even found a rotting log full of ants and grubs teeming in the thawed and pulpy sapwood, and these, too, the bear and the girl enjoyed with their supper.

And when night fell and the stars came out, the bear curled up against the trunk of an old white pine while the girl gathered needles in a heap next to him for her bed. She lay there for a long time, smelling the sweet scent of ground mixed with the fur smell of bear. She felt at home there, watching Virgo and Sagittarius, the hunter, drift across the sky. She lay awake most of the night, listening to the songs of mockingbirds and the hoot of an owl, until she drifted off in the early hours of dawn, and no dreams followed her.

THE SUN SHONE HIGH IN THE SKY WHEN THE bear shook the girl awake the next day and said, It's time to fish.

They weren't far from the river. As they emerged from the woods, they could see the forest and hills to the west and hear the sound of the rushing water as they drew closer.

The bear seemed stronger each waking day, but when they came to the water's edge, he dived into the swift current and went under so fast and for so long, the girl thought he had been washed away. She stripped herself of bow and quiver and was about to dive in after him, when she saw him reemerge several strides downstream, a big trout slapping back and forth in his jaws as he struggled to regain his footing and climb ashore.

He walked back to the girl and stood sopping wet in front of her, the trout still flopping about in his mouth. He dropped it in the grass, and said, You were right.

The girl eyed the bear and said, You're the one who said everything speaks. Do you think all those fish know there's a hungry bear around? What do we do now?

The bear said nothing, just sat on the ground and devoured his trout. When he was finished, he got back on all fours, and asked the girl, Would you like one?

I can get my own, she said.

She picked up her bow, took a fishing arrow from her quiver, and stepped gently into the current. She could see the water had gone down a great deal since the days when it was nothing but an ice floe, but it was still fast and dangerous. The rock from which she had fished previously was in the path of where the bear had fished, so she walked upstream and scanned the surface current for evidence of a similar pattern of boulders on the river bottom. She had gone no fewer than twenty strides upriver before she found one and waded slowly out to it as though she were stalking game over land.

The bear followed at a distance from shore. He had never seen anything in the forest gather fish with a bow and arrow before. But there was the girl, perched on a rock just below the surface, peering into the water that rushed in two separate moons around the right and left sides of her. She stood as still and silent as a kingfisher the bear had often seen in creeks and swamps in his travels, until she raised her bow, drew back, and released. The line stripped out from the bow and stopped. The girl tugged and began to retrieve it hand over hand, and on the other end of it there was a fish.

She held her own trout up by the mouth for the bear to see. He threw his head back in a nod of appreciation and waded downstream to continue fishing on his own.

THE GIRL AND THE BEAR NEVER RETURNED TO the mountain cave. They lived on the riverbank for several phases of the moon that spring, fishing and foraging for ostrich ferns, wild leeks, anything they could find in the abundance of the ground. They walked in the forest together, if the girl needed to find wood with which to fashion a new arrow, or if the bear felt a desire to climb. And often on these walks the girl would tell the bear things her father had told her about the earth, the sun, the moon, and the oceans. And when they sat around their fire at night, they wondered together what it might be like to be on another part of the earth, or to cross an entire ocean.

WHEN THE SNOW HAD MELTED EVERYWHERE BUT in the high mountains, the two set off together for the north. The girl to the place where she would cross the river and carry the remains of her father home. The bear to travel with her, and to listen to her stories, some of which she had heard from her father, others she made up when she had exhausted her memory and the bear asked for more.

One night around a fire on a small mountain lake in which slabs of ice still floated like islands unmoored, the girl asked the bear how long he had been wandering through the forest, and how long he yet hoped to wander.

It has been some time, said the bear. More summers than I have toes. We're given that many years plus ten before we don't wake up from winter.

The girl sat and stared into the fire.

You don't know how many you are given, do you? asked the bear.

No, said the girl.

The bear looked through the fire at the girl and said, as though this would settle the question, The trees will know.

FOR MUCH OF THEIR TRAVELS THEY WALKED AND climbed through rain and lay down to sleep at night beneath rock overhangs or thick pine branches, wet and without a fire, only to rise and continue on. The girl did not care and neither did the bear. They had food, and that was all that seemed to matter.

When finally they came to the rocks where the girl had crossed the river with her father, the two remained in the grove closest to the roar of the stream and camped there for several warm, dry days, fishing for the small brook trout that lurked deep in the pools and smoking the fish so the girl would have food with which to travel on the final leg of her journey home. And on a night when a full moon rose in the eastern sky, the girl told the bear she had reckoned from her marks on the cave wall that the solstice would fall on the last full moon of the spring. The one that would come around after this one had waned to new.

The bear nodded and was quiet, and the girl asked him if he would travel to the mountain that stands alone with her.

It's your home, he said to the girl, and she understood this meant no.

What will you do? she asked.

I'm a bear, he said. I'll wander.

And that night they built the fire up as high as it would go and sat around it, the bear this time telling the girl the stories that not only his mother but other bears with which he had crossed paths had told him, stories when others like the girl lived in every corner of the earth, and stories from long, long ago, when there were only a few. And of the beginning, when there was no one, and the forests and oceans and all the earth was new.

In the morning, the bear was gone. The girl cooked the last of the fish and warmed a cup

of tea for her breakfast over a fire stoked with
the limbs she had used to make her smoke rack.
After she had finished her food, she tarried by
the fire, letting the sticks burn, smelling the
wood smoke and fresh fir in the air, wondering which direction she would take if she were
a bear. And when the fire was only embers, she
placed two of them in her tin cup stuffed with
green leaves and covered the charcoal and ash
in the pit with dirt and pushed pine needles all
around so that it looked as though no one or
no thing had ever done more than pass through
that grove. Then she picked up her bow, quiver,
and pack and walked to the edge of the river.

THE AIR WARMED AND HINTS OF SUMMER were on the breeze as she traveled south. Young birds at first flight. Doe-watched fawns in the brush. Wild strawberries small and sweet ripening in mountain meadows. She measured the length of her shadow each day as she went and found she had kept her calendar correctly. She saw landmarks she remembered from when she had passed through with her father, and then the new crescent moon.

She traveled on, up and down summits and through valleys, sleeping in the shelter of groves when she could see nothing before her, and rising before the sun to make the most of daylight. She had long ago eaten the last of the smoked fish and now ate the plants of the forest, as she and her father had done, not wanting to shoot game that would have its young close by. Nor did she make any fires.

She moved southward, and on a morning with

a clear sky and the last of a waxing moon setting in the west while an orange sun rose in the east, the girl looked out from the vista on which she stood and recognized in the distance the unmistakable headlike summit of the mountain that stands alone, a full day's hike away. She shouldered her pack and walked back into the canopy of trees and headed down into the valley in the direction of home.

THE HOUSE LOOKED JUST AS THEY HAD LEFT IT but for the signs of winter. Broken pine limbs and piles of needles littered the roof and covered the porch and doorway like a mat. A birch spotted with woodpecker holes had broken at its base and fallen onto the toolshed at the edge of the woods, and as she approached to climb the stone steps that led to the front door, a raccoon fled with her gaze of kits.

Though the day was warming, the house was cold inside. The hearth swept clean a year ago was piled with leaves stained with guano, and the table, too, was littered with the droppings of mice and chipmunks. She pulled a book of poems from the small shelf on which it sat and the cover came off in her hands and she put it back. She looked about and walked into the room where her father had slept and found it as before, but for the stillness and the spiderwebs. The bow with which he had hunted lay on the bed, where he had left it. The hammock he used to string between two trees down by the lakeshore hung from a hook on the wall. She took the hammock, walked back into the kitchen, and left the house.

SHE WOKE BEFORE DAWN THE NEXT DAY AND ATE nothing for her breakfast. From the collapsed shed she took a pickax and an iron bar and, with her pack still on her back and the compass in her hand, she began to walk to the top of the mountain before the sun had even risen.

Where the path came out of the trees, she turned and saw the shingled roof of the small house and waited on the trail for the sound of footfalls approaching over the stone, but she heard nothing and no one. She gazed up at the summit and strode the rest of the way toward it.

At her mother's grave, she placed her hand

on top of the flat marker as she had always done, though this time so that it would steady her and hold her up as she swayed in the constant wind and looked out over the land from which she had come. She took a drink of water from the gourd, slid the pack from her back, and placed it on the ground. She untied the pickax and held it in both hands, walked a few paces away from her mother's grave, and began to swing it hard into the rock and dirt.

THE SUN WAS ARCING INTO THE WEST WHEN SHE had finished hammering and digging a hole in that earth. She knelt down, opened her pack, and took out the skin, untied it, and looked once more on the bones and ashes of her father. Then she rolled the skin up again, placed it into the grave, and pushed the dirt back into the hole with her hands until all that she had held of the man was covered and gone.

Now come the days when I'll miss you.

She stood and stepped back and looked at the scree that formed a small mound on the ground and felt all of a sudden what the man had told her he had felt when he had buried the woman. Though rain and snow would be the only things to touch him in that ground, still she wanted nothing to disturb him. So she set out collecting stones of the same size and with the hours that made up that longest day she erected four walls around the perimeter of the grave, the course and wythe six long and six high, set without perpend of any kind. Then she began to fill the inside one by one with whatever rocks and small boulders she could lift and carry, until the area within was filled except for a hollow in the middle. Into this she placed the compass and covered it with a flat slab of gneiss, the striations of which reminded her of the waves in the sea.

IT WAS A LONG TIME BEFORE DARKNESS FELL AND stars began to wheel across the sky. And though a night wind whipped against her face and body on the mountain, there was a warmth to it she had not felt since she last stood there on the longest day of the year and let her clothes and sweat dry. She was hungry and she was tired, but she did not want to leave them. The wind blew north to south across the summit and she crouched down between the cover of both graves and laid on that stone and in that silence alone, a girl no longer, though forever their child.

IN HER FINAL YEARS, THE OLD WOMAN SPOKE to all of the living things of the earth between the mountain and the lakeshore, for they came to her without fear of dominion and ate with her the plants and seeds and fruits she grew and picked. She never saw the bear again, nor did she cease to wonder how and where he had been even after she knew the span of his own life had long come to an end.

She had for many seasons ceased to climb the mountain on which remained the graves of her parents. In winter, she slept in a cave on the island and fished through the ice. And from early spring to the edge of autumn, she moved back to the lakeshore and slept on the ground or in a hammock she would weave from vines and string between the trunks of the same two towering white pines.

She no longer went inside the house. The ruined books, the leather-bound tablets of paper

on which she once wrote, and the wooden fur-
niture her father had made had all fed fires that
warmed her on cool nights of early spring and late
autumn. The window glass was broken and scattered along the floor. The roof and walls slouched
and buckled and became unsound, until she came
back from the island one spring and found that
these, too, had fallen in, and she burned the timber and shakes piece by piece in her fire.

Each morning, she rose as though from the
earth, then lay down to sleep again when the
sun had set and the only lights were the stars
in the dome of the sky. In the winter, she had
time to sit among the beech and pines on the
island and listen to their whispering. In summer, when she walked to the lake, it was to wash
her old and naked body in the cool depths of
the water, accompanied by the song of the gray
catbird and the cry of the loon, as she had been
most of her life. And when she came out of the
water and sat down on the grass by the rock that
held the noon mark her father had placed there
long ago, it was to sit and listen still to the slow
and susurrant voice of the trees.

ON THE NIGHT OF A HARVEST MOON IN AUTUMN, the soft breezes to which she went to sleep in summer now blowing throughout the evening like a wind, she took her last breath and in the morning lay at rest on the dew-covered ground. She remained there untouched throughout the fall and winter under a blanket of leaves and snow, and she lay there in the spring when the snows melted and shoots of grass, wildflowers, and young maples grew around and through her soft and sunken body.

AND THERE CAME TO THE LAKESHORE ON THE first day of summer a bear who had been told to journey to a mountain that stands alone, and when he arrived, he saw what he had been told of in the stories passed down to him by the dam bear from the moment she licked the birth from his eyes. And he understood what it was he had promised to do.

He gathered up a mat of broken boughs of spruce and placed in it the woman's bones and leathery remains and carried them to the top of the mountain. There he lifted rocks and dug in the earth with his claws and laid the blanket in that earth between a flat stone table and a block of four walls. When he had finished, the dirt and shards of stones he had unearthed barely covered the sacking of pine in which the old woman lay and made poor cover for a grave. It was then he saw the outcropping near the summit that looked faintly like the cracked and eroded head of those like him he had encountered in his travels. He ambled toward it, walked around its perimeter, then rose on his hind legs and pushed. The stone gave way and rolled off the shoulder of the summit in the direction of the three graves. And the bear rolled that headstone the final distance to its resting place over the woman he had come to bury.

IT HAD BEEN NIGHT A LONG TIME WHEN HE emerged from the trees and lumbered into the clearing beneath a waning moon. He waded into the lake, drank, then came out, sat in the high grass, and looked up at the stars. He felt the fatigue of his task, as though he had come to a place where end and beginning were the same, and in the time he had spent on that mountain everything had changed. He lifted his ears to listen and heard nothing. No steps of animals. No whisper of trees. No snap of insects. No lapping waves. A silence as cold and strange to him as winter. He wondered how long he had been sitting there, if for just a moment the earth stood still, when the leaves of the forest began to rustle, and the ghostly wail of a loon floated across the surface of the water. He rose and stretched and turned so that the Great Bear was over his right shoulder. Then he set out, moving west along the shore, the sky beginning to pale behind him like the world itself being born.

BELLEVUE LITERARY PRESS is devoted to publishing literary fiction and nonfiction at the intersection of the arts and sciences because we believe that science and the humanities are natural companions for understanding the human experience. With each book we publish, our goal is to foster a rich, interdisciplinary dialogue that will forge new tools for thinking and engaging with the world.

To support our press and its mission, and for our full catalogue of published titles, please visit us at blpress.org.

BELLEVUE LITERARY PRESS
New York